# LENNY CYRUS
## SCHOOL VIRUS

### JOE SCHREIBER

ILLUSTRATED BY

### MATT SMITH

**HOUGHTON MIFFLIN**
**HOUGHTON MIFFLIN HARCOURT**
**BOSTON NEW YORK**

Houghton Mifflin is an imprint of
Houghton Mifflin Harcourt Publishing Company.

www.hmhbooks.com

The text of this book is set in Caecilia LT.
The illustrations are digital.

*Library of Congress Cataloging-in-Publication Data*
Schreiber, Joe, 1969–

Lenny Cyrus, school virus / by Joe Schreiber.

p. cm.

Summary: Told from three viewpoints, thirteen-year-old scientific genius Lenny
Cyrus shrinks himself and, helped by his best friend Harlan, enters the body of
Zooey, the girl he has loved since third grade, hoping to physically change her mind
about him on the very day her play opens.

ISBN 978-0-547-89315-0

[1. Interpersonal relations—Fiction. 2. Middle schools—Fiction. 3. Schools—Fiction. 4.
Size—Fiction. 5. Human body—Fiction. 6. Theater—Fiction.] I. Title.

PZ7.S37913Len 2013

[Fic]—dc23

2012034048


Printed in the United States of America
DOC 10 9 8 7 6 5 4 3 2
4500415380

*TO JACK, THE BOY WHO CHANGED EVERYTHING.*

# ::: *PROLOGUE* :::

It had taken me five years, but I'd finally found my way to Zooey Andrews's heart. Now I was going to die there.

The world around me felt like it was shaking itself to pieces, the deafening thump and whoosh of blood roaring through the great vessels, spinning me around in a whirlpool, sucking away whatever remained of my equilibrium.

I knew that if I had thirty seconds to think about it, to analyze the data, I could figure this out. But I didn't. It wasn't supposed to end this way. Not at all.

*I'm sorry, Zooey.*

Everything tightened, and I felt the elastic bands of cardiac muscle shaking like a runaway roller coaster. White blood cells came bursting through, crowding my vision, sticky white leukocytes lunging forward from all sides in a swarm of doomed immunity. Who could've guessed that the heart of a fourteen-year-old girl was such a violent place?

My back was to the wall of the left ventricle. It was a little over a centimeter thick, but it might as well have been made of reinforced concrete. There was no place to run. After less than six hours inside Zooey's system,

I'd almost managed to kill her. Now she was returning the favor.

I guess we weren't meant to be together after all.

Oh well.

You can't blame a guy for trying.

# ONE ::: LENNY

Love and science don't mix.

You could say that I should've known that from the start, and you'd probably be right, but it wouldn't change the way that I felt about Zooey. I'd been in love with her since the day we first met, and in a way, everything I ever did, everything I ever dreamed of achieving, was all for her.

I'd known her since third grade when she saved my butt on the playground. A kid named Mick Mason had been teasing me, trying to pick a fight for some reason. Maybe he didn't like the color of my backpack. Maybe it was because it was a Monday, or the cafeteria had served fish sticks that day. Who knows? Whatever it was, he finally got sick of waiting and just started punching. He had me pinned me down under the tetherball post and landed two or three good hits when a hand with chipped pink fingernail polish grabbed him and hauled him off.

I looked up. The dark-haired presence in jeans and a vintage Nirvana T-shirt was hovering over me, early-afternoon sunlight blazing from behind her. She reached down and helped me up, brushing the black crumbs of asphalt from my cheek and looking at me strangely.

"Are you crying?"

"What? No. No. I'm just . . . sweating."

"From your eyes?"

I gazed at her, unable to speak. I was only eight years old, but I knew true beauty when I saw it. She had smooth hair that swung down past her shoulders and the kind of scratchy voice that made it sound like she'd just stopped laughing or was about to start again. Behind her glasses, her eyes were that pure methylene blue that you only see in perfectly balanced chemical solutions.

Zooey smiled. "So, you're okay?"

"Yeah," I said. "Thanks. My name's—"

"Lenny Cyrus," she said. "I know."

"You . . ." The sting of the attack disappeared instantly in a warm buzz of disbelief. "You know my name?"

"Well, yeah."

From that moment on, all the kids in school talked about me in a whole new way.

*: : :*

*"Lenny Cyrus got saved by a girl!"*

You'd think that something like that would only last a few days, a couple weeks at the most, definitely no more than a month, until people found something more interesting to talk about. At least that's what my mom and dad said.

"The average attention span of a third-grader is six seconds," my father said from behind his laptop. It was dinnertime, and he was typing an e-mail in between bites of chicken Kiev. "Trust me, they'll move on to something else before you know it."

"Listen to your father." That was my mom, from behind *her* laptop, on the other side of the table, clicking away even faster while she picked at her salad. "He knows what it's like to be ostracized by his peers." She glanced up at him. "Remember the Gluck fellowship, honey?"

"Don't remind me," Dad said, reaching over to touch her hand.

She smiled. "Poor baby."

My parents always talked that way. They'd been high school sweethearts, and the two things they had in common were that a) after sixteen years of marriage they were both still crazy in love, and b) they were both geniuses. And by that, I don't mean that they were just, you know, *really smart*. They were both adjunct professors at the University of Chicago, they had IQs of 194 and 187 (Dad never quite forgave Mom for those extra seven points), with a total of six doctorates, three newly discovered subatomic particles, and the shared Nobel Prize for physics for their work "in helping discover the mechanism of spontaneous broken symmetry on the microscopic level." We had an x-ray crystallography rig in the basement and a pulsar timing array on the roof, next to the Santa Claus sled and reindeer that Dad had forgotten to take down after Christmas. Merging supermassive black holes had always been one of Dad's weekend hobbies, along with Civil War relics and home brewing.

So, when it came to my problems at school, I did what any kid with genius parents would have done.

I listened to them.

It turned out to be a huge mistake. Not only did Zooey Andrews and I *not* become friends after what happened on the playground, but she stopped talking to me completely. At the end of fourth grade, she got new glasses, big black-framed ones, which somehow made her look even prettier. She'd started sitting off in the corner of the cafeteria by herself, writing in black spiral notebooks, glancing up once in a while to make sure that the world hadn't changed in any profound way while she'd been finishing her last sentence. In sixth grade, she joined the drama club and helped build sets and make costumes for the middle school play, *Mary Poppins*, and I kept wondering what she was really working on in those notebooks.

Meanwhile, I just disappeared.

It wasn't on purpose. I won the regional science fair, got my picture in the paper for the model cold-fusion reactor that I built in my garage, and helped a high school quarterback who was five years older than me get through basic math—but I couldn't change my status to save my life. By the end of seventh grade, I had sprouted up four inches and was one of the tallest kids in my class, but it didn't matter. I was so radioactive that most of the kids in school didn't even bother picking on me except when some overgrown glandular case had to release some testosterone. I had completely faded into the realm of the invisible, lost among the misfits whose freakishness was so extreme that it was just easier to pretend they didn't exist.

My parents seemed to think all this was good news.

"I know you don't understand this now," my mom said one night, as she and Dad were finishing their application for research time on Brookhaven's polarized proton collider, "but someday when you're on the cover of *Newsweek*, advising the president on how to solve the energy crisis, you'll look back on middle school and smile."

That wasn't what I wanted. I was going to be fourteen in April, with the rest of my teenage years stretching out in front of me like the endless desert of an atomic test site. I thought about Zooey Andrews.

Being invisible wasn't enough anymore.

"Any other advice?"

"Just be yourself, honey," my mom said. "Trust me, if this Zephyr person is worth the effort—"

"Zooey, Mom."

"—Right. If she's worth your time, then she'll eventually realize how special you really are."

My best friend, Harlan, had another way of putting it.

"You just have to do something so cool that even Zooey can't deny its awesomeness." We were walking down the hall on the way to the cafeteria, which, according to Harlan, was where he did his best thinking. He had a Mountain Dew in one hand and a Snickers bar in the other.

"That's not very helpful," I said. "Anything more specific?"

"Start small. Maybe try freezing the whole school so we all get to go home early or something."

"Yeah, right," I said. Harlan definitely wasn't stupid, but he wasn't exactly a rocket scientist either. He listened to hip-hop, rode a skateboard, and had lived down the street from me since we were in kindergarten. In fact, he was shockingly normal. The weirdest thing about him, besides his ability to make tropical bird noises in the back of social studies class, was that in spite of everything I'd done, he was still my best friend.

I looked up the hallway and stopped.

"Uh-oh."

Up ahead, I saw Mick Mason and one of his lackeys change direction and start heading toward us at what my brain automatically calculated as a perfect fifty-two-degree angle. The moment they saw us—saw *me*—a predatory glint flashed through Mick's expression. Anybody who doubts that middle school is like a Discovery Channel documentary on natural selection just hasn't been paying attention.

Harlan skimmed between them without even noticing they were there, but when I tried to follow, Mick and his pal both came in close, popped out their elbows, and jammed them into my ribs from either side as they passed. By the time Harlan realized what had happened and turned around, they were gone.

"Lenny, are you all right?"

"I'm . . . fine." My rib cage felt like it had been popped open with giant set of nutcrackers, but I didn't see any need to tell him that.

Harlan glanced back. "Did those guys do something to you, Lenny?"

"No, I'm good," I managed. "You were saying something about . . . freezing the school?"

"Yeah, or maybe, like . . . send it back in time, or something." He shrugged and stepped into the lunch line. "You're the genius. You'll figure something out."

Twenty minutes later, as we were sitting in the computer lab, killing time before the next class, I came across the answer.

"Harlan, check this out."

"The Singer Prize?" He squinted at the screen, barely distracted from the page of dirt bikes and ATVs that he'd been checking out. "Never heard of it."

"Every year the U.S. Department of Education gives an award for the greatest scientific achievement by a middle school student." I grabbed a quick breath. Sometimes when I talk fast, I forget to breathe. "It is, hands down, the most prestigious award in the middle school scientific community."

"Dude." Harlan looked at me. "You're going to win Zooey over with a science project?"

"*Dude,*" I said, imitating him, "the kid who won last year got to have dinner with the president."

"Seriously?"

"They flew him to the White House on Air Force One." I actually wasn't sure about that last part, but the visual of me stepping off the jet at Dulles International and gazing out at a crowd of reporters with Zooey Andrews on my arm as a plus-one was too good to resist.

"Okay," Harlan admitted, "that might do it. If you could come up with the right idea."

"No problem," I said. "I've already got it."

## *TWO ::: HARLAN*

Two things you need to know about my friend Lenny.

    1. He is a genius.

    2. He's a total tool.

He can't help it. *You* try growing up with two Nobel Prize–winning scientists sitting across the breakfast table from you. Lenny doesn't like to talk about it, but he's at least as smart as his mom and dad, probably smarter. And let's face it: You can't be that smart without being extremely dumb in other ways. It's like the universe strapped this jet-pack on his back, then Gorilla-glued his sneakers to the floor. He's constantly reaching out too far and falling flat on his face.

Sometimes it's painful to watch.

Like the time he decided to bury my uncle's old camper in my backyard and turn it into a groundhog colony, complete with underground video cameras—until the groundhogs started gnawing on the wires and

electrocuting themselves, blacking out the whole neighborhood in the process. Or his garage gene-splicing experiment, when he was ten years old, where he tried to use a box turtle to fertilize a frog's egg. He got the idea from an old *Ripley's Believe It or Not* paperback he found in my basement. I still remember the crushed look on his face as he stood there with the stethoscope around his neck and that dead egg in his hands.

His brain was supercharged. He had a photographic memory and he could memorize entire college textbooks in an hour or less, and understand everything he'd read. Someday his heart and his feelings were going to catch up to his brain, but it was going to take some time. I had no doubt that if Zooey Andrews could just see what he was going to be like in fifteen years—curing cancer and patching up the ozone layer, or whatever—she'd fall in love with him on general principles. He was one in a million. He was destined for greatness. Everybody knows that it pays to keep guys like him around and happy.

But when Zooey finally did pay attention to us, it wasn't in the way that any of us expected.

"Harlan?"

I was standing in the doorway outside homeroom, trying to decide whether I needed one more Mountain Dew to get through Mr. Grant's algebra class, when I noticed Zooey coming over to me with her usual morning Diet Coke. Aria Keen was standing next to her with an iPad, on which, I could see, she was reading the *Hollywood Reporter*.

"Oh," I said, "hey."

"What's going on?" Zooey asked.

"Not much," I said. "What's up with you?"

"I need your help," she said, and took a sip from the bottle. "The fate of the universe depends on it."

I faked a yawn. "Is that all?"

"Uh-huh." She glanced up over her shoulder at the poster hanging between a row of lockers and a fire extinguisher. It showed a big white North Pole landscape with a single bloody footprint in the snow, a red Santa cap underneath it. Across the top, in dripping red letters, it said:

# YOU'D BETTER WATCH OUT.

And underneath the picture, in slightly smaller letters:

## ESCAPE CLAUS
### Written and directed by Zooey Andrews
### December 7th–9th, 15th–16th
### 3:30 and 7:00 p.m.
### Cosgrove Middle School Auditorium

*Escape Claus* was Zooey's play—she'd finished the script back in seventh grade, but it had taken a year to persuade the school board to let her produce it, which wasn't a surprise, considering the subject matter.

"A few days before Christmas," Zooey had told the school paper, "the army receives a distress signal from the North Pole. They send a team of commandos to check it out, and they find Santa's workshop, but the whole place seems abandoned. Doors are torn down, windows are broken, and snow is blowing and drifting across piles of broken toys. As they explore the workshop, they realize something terrible has happened. There's something wrong with Santa. He's been infected by some kind of virus in the ice that's turned him into a monster. Our heroes have twenty-four hours to cure him, fix the toy shop, and save Christmas . . . if they can—*Escape Claus.*"

It was a musical. Zooey had spent two years writing the play. The decision to add music and lyrics was partly because of Aria, who was captain of the Cosgrove Middle School Songleaders and refused to be in any production that didn't allow her to sing. The school board wasn't all that thrilled about Zooey putting on a Christmas play with an evil Santa Claus to begin with, but apparently adding music made a difference. She said there's a musical called *Sweeney Todd* that does the same thing, and that one's about a guy who turns people into meat pies.

"What's wrong?" I asked Zooey. "Did the principal finally get cold feet and yank your funding?"

"Hardly," Aria said. "Our play is the best thing that's happened to this school in a long time."

"Well," Zooey said, "I wouldn't go that far. But things are going well." Then, with a little frown: "Or at least they were, until now."

In my pocket, my phone started to play the ringtone

for "She Blinded Me with Science," which meant that Lenny was calling me. I ignored it. It was ten minutes to eight, and kids were starting to head to their first-period classes. Lenny would be looking for me, probably trying to find out if I'd bring him a SmartWater. His brain didn't need caffeine like mine did, but he was an electrolyte fiend.

"So what's the problem?" I asked.

"Here, hold this." She had already gotten out a measuring tape and was unrolling it in front of me. "Keep this up by your head. That's it."

"Wait," I said. "What—"

"Stop fidgeting." She squatted down to line up the bottom of the measuring tape with my shoes. "Five-seven." And then, wrapping the tape around my waist: "Twenty-four-inch waist. Thirty-inch chest . . ." Glancing up at me with a pencil in her teeth: "Anybody ever tell you that you're built like a ballerina, Williams?"

"Zooey, what are you doing?"

"What's it look like?" She glanced at Aria, who was typing notes on her iPad. "That's close enough, isn't it?"

Aria nodded but didn't look especially happy about it. "It's going to have to be. We can make modifications if we have to."

"Whoa," I said, backing away. "What's going on here?"

"Weren't you listening? We need your help."

"What, for the play? Zooey, I can't act. And I definitely can't sing."

"But you're five-seven, which means you can fit the suit," Zooey said, "and right now that's what matters."

"What suit?" I looked at her, finally beginning to understand. "Wait," I said, "you mean . . ."

"That's right."

"But I thought Ryan Forrester—"

"Ryan Forrester is out with a raging case of mono," Zooey said. "Which puts you at the top of a very short list." She smiled, the pencil still in her mouth, and I noticed it was a real smile, the kind that made her eyes sparkle around the edges. Why hadn't I noticed how pretty she was before now? "Don't worry, there are barely any lines. Nobody will even see your face."

"Okay." I took in a breath and let it out. "Here's the thing. I'm, like, really flattered and everything . . ."

Zooey took the pencil out of her mouth and stared at me. "Flattered?" she asked, eyebrows up, but smiling a little, like she couldn't believe her ears. "He says he's flattered, Aria."

"I heard him."

I took in another deep breath. "Like I said, I appreciate the offer . . ."

"But?"

"But I think . . . you know, maybe there might be somebody else who would do an even better job at it than I would."

"Who's that?"

"Lenny Cyrus."

Zooey and Aria both blinked at me. The smile slipped away from Zooey's face, while Aria, who had never been smiling, began to actively frown.

"Lenny Cyrus?" Zooey said.

"Look, just—hear me out, okay?" Sensing that I was already losing her, I started to talk faster. "Lenny Cyrus is a nice guy. And plus, he's tall. Taller than I am, probably, by at least an inch. Why don't you ask him?"

She didn't say anything. Next to her, Aria rolled her eyes and looked like she might throw up or slip into a coma or both.

"Lenny Cyrus doesn't even talk to me," Zooey said quietly. "He doesn't even look at me in the hallway."

"He's shy."

"Which isn't exactly what I'm looking for on stage."

"He can't help the way he is," I said. "Who knows? Maybe this will be good for him. You know, build his confidence or whatever?"

"This isn't a self-help seminar," Aria said. "We've got a show to do. We open in less than a week. Right now we just need what's good for the production. And what's good for the production . . ." she leaned forward and tapped me in the middle of my thirty-inch chest— "is you."

"Hold on a second, Ar." Zooey was still thinking. "Maybe there is something that Lenny could help us with. If he wanted to. I mean, I'm certainly not going to force him, but . . ."

I was thinking that Zooey probably wouldn't have to force Lenny to do anything that involved spending time with her when my phone buzzed again, like a warning bell. Up the hall, I saw Mick Mason coming my way, followed by his friends Keegan Hoke and Deke Chambers. Mick had noticed that Zooey and Aria were talking to me, and now the three of them came drifting over with all the slyness of a pack of hyenas.

"Hey, *Har-lan*." He leaned in close enough that I could smell his breath. "Where's your little girlfriend?"

"You might want to go home and brush your teeth again, Mick," I told him. "I can still smell the toxic waste you ate for breakfast."

"How about I knock a few of yours out instead, jerknuts?"

Zooey sighed. "What do you want, Mick?"

"Just spreading some Christmas cheer." Mick yanked a roll of stickers from his jacket pocket and slapped one on Aria's shoulder and the other on Zooey's sweater. Aria's sticker read NAUGHTY. Zooey's said NICE. Behind him, Keegan and Deke sniggered like this was the funniest thing they'd ever seen.

"Well," Aria said, grimacing, "spread it somewhere else." She wadded up the sticker and flicked it back at him.

Mick looked at her with a weird mingling of surprise and anger but didn't say anything. His eyes narrowed as he tried to kick the crumpled sticker into the corner of the hall. It stuck to the toe of his boot until he finally had to bend over to peel it off.

Meanwhile Zooey had grabbed my arm and dragged

me over to the corner. "Well?" she said. "Are you going to help me or not?"

I realized that she was just going to keep after me, waiting for an answer, and finally found myself nodding along, not because I *wanted* to dress as a giant evil Santa—the suit Zooey had built for the production was its best special effect—but because I didn't feel like I had much of a choice. I'd been swept up in the rush of her enthusiasm. For a slightly nerdy girl with a ponytail and glasses, she had a kind of magnetic force, and after a while you just felt yourself getting sucked in.

"And tell Lenny," she added, "that we could use his help too. But there's not much time—we open on Friday afternoon."

"Tick-tock," Aria muttered, and twisted the gold doorknocker earring dangling from her left ear.

"*Lenny?*" Mick grunted, and stiffened up as if he'd just been hit with a cattle prod. "What's that dorkwad got to do with anything?"

Zooey kept pretending he didn't exist and walked off. I smiled at her and tried not to notice as Mick and his buddies gave me one last glare, then turned and followed after her and Aria. As soon as Zooey turned the corner, I pulled out my phone and looked at the screen. It was a text message from Lenny, all right, but he wasn't asking me to bring him a SmartWater.

The message read:

*Meet me in the science lab. RIGHT NOW.*

::::

"Hey, man," I said, stepping into the lab, "I'm already gonna be late for class. We're not all lucky enough to have independent study, you know."

Lenny didn't even look up from his microscope. He was wearing a white lab coat that was too short in the sleeves and standing behind the counter in the otherwise empty lab that our biology teacher, Dr. Snyder, let him use during free period. It made his schedule a lot more flexible, so he was able to help me with my homework.

"Harlan," Lenny said, "you need to see this."

"Did you even hear what I said?"

He didn't answer, just made some small adjustment to the microscope. On the metal shelves behind him, white rats rustled in their cages and rattled their water bottles. One of the cages was empty, the lid leaning up against its side, but at the time it didn't occur to me to wonder where the occupants were. Lenny was always getting the rats out and playing with them, or just letting them scurry around the lab while he worked.

"Listen, Lenny," I said. "There's something I have to tell you. I was outside of homeroom this morning, and—"

"Harlan, I did it." He straightened up, his face flushed with excitement. "It works."

I glanced at him. "What?"

"See for yourself. I'm a shoe-in for the Singer Prize. As soon as I'm finished here I'm going to ask Dr. Snyder to write my letter of recommendation. And once Zooey hears about it—"

"That's actually kind of what I wanted to—"

"Check it out. I mean, it's crazy, and it's not supposed to work, but it totally *does*." He turned and pointed at the blackboard, which was crammed with equations that I wouldn't have been able to decipher in a million years. Then he started talking very quickly, barely catching his breath, the way he did when an idea had taken hold and wouldn't let him go. "Okay, so you know what Planck's Constant is, right?"

"Uh . . ."

Lenny rolled his eyes. "It's a physical constant reflecting the size of quanta in quantum mechanics."

"Okay."

"Harlan, if you're not even going to *try* to understand—"

"Okay," I said, "I just think you'd better hear what I have to say first, all right?"

"I reduced it."

"You reduced it, that's great."

"Yeah, I reduced Planck's Constant. See, you're not supposed to be able to *do* that, but . . ." He just stared at me, rubbing his hands together, waiting for me to congratulate him. "You still don't get it, do you?"

"Lenny, Zooey Andrews just—"

"Just look for yourself," he said, and pointed at the microscope.

"Fine." More to shut him up than anything else, I leaned in and looked through the eyepiece at the petrie dish.

And I forgot all about Zooey Andrews.

I stared through the lens, unable to believe what I was seeing.

The little things scurrying around in the petrie dish were rats.

Tiny microscopic white rats. With little whiskers, little pink tails, and little twitching noses. I stood there watching them for a second, then stood up and looked back at Lenny and the empty cage sitting beside him.

"You did that?" I said.

"I did that."

"You shrank the lab rats?"

"Uh-huh." He was grinning and nodding his head, reminding me of the time when he was six years old and had discovered how to open every garage door in our neighborhood using the rewired stereo equipment in his dad's Oldsmobile.

"How small are they?"

"Between six and eight micrometers," he said. "About the size of a bacteria cell."

"How . . . I mean . . ." For a second I was at a loss for words. "Holy cow, Lenny. That's . . . *amazing*. Even for you."

"I know, right?"

"How did you—"

"I already told you."

I glanced back up at the briar patch of equations on the blackboard. "You reduced Planck's Constant."

"It's simple chemistry—a basic application of nano-technology, actually. Once I was able to miniaturize the individual atoms in their bodies, I used a modified virology algorithm to encase them in a protein sheath, and—"

"A protein shake?"

"A *sheath*," Lenny said, but for once he didn't sound exasperated. "The point is, for all intents and purposes, though they are miniature rats, they move and behave like benign viruses. They're alive. They're perfectly healthy. Their little lungs can even draw oxygen directly from the hemoglobin sample on the slide. They're just extremely small."

"But . . . they're rats." I glanced one more time at the wall-size snarl of equations on the chalkboard, none of it making any more sense than it had a second earlier, and then back at the empty cage. "*Those* rats."

"Uh-huh."

"Those exact rats, which were in that cage this morning."

"Yep."

"Has anybody ever—"

"Nope."

"Lenny," I said, and now I was starting to get excited, "we have to call the news. Tell somebody. Tell *everybody*. This is amazing."

"What's so amazing?" a voice asked behind me, and we both turned around to see Zooey Andrews step into the science lab.

# THREE ::: ZOOEY

In her memoir *Lunching with Sharks*, the Academy Award–winning producer Martha Gelhorn-Smith, one of the most powerful women in Hollywood, provides a list of ten rules to succeed in the movie industry.

*Rule #3: Close the deal at all costs.*

I went to the science lab because I needed to close the deal with Harlan. It was that simple. I needed him to wear the Santa suit, because if he didn't, then we didn't have a Santa, and without a Santa, we didn't have a play.

And that couldn't happen.

I had worked too hard—building sets, making props, sewing costumes, putting up with Aria, rehearsing and practicing, writing and rewriting—for it to fall apart now, all because Ryan Forrester got mono.

So even though the late bell was about to ring, I grabbed my books and made a run for the science lab.

When I walked into the lab, trying to act like I wasn't breathing hard, Harlan and Lenny were both standing next to one of the microscopes, wearing guilty expressions, as if I'd caught them spying on something. But that was crazy, even for Lenny. Who spies on germs?

"Oh, hey, Zooey," Harlan said. "Long time no see."

"Hello, Harlan." I looked at Lenny. "Hi, Lenny."

Lenny looked up at me and made a gurgling noise, as if he was trying to clear his throat but couldn't quite do it. "Hello, Zooey." He looked down at my chest. "Oh, nice."

"Excuse me?" Glancing down, I realized that the NICE sticker that Mick had slapped onto my sweater was still there. "Oh. That." I ripped it off and crumpled it up. *Rule #8: When negotiating, act like you already have everything you want and you're doing the other person a favor just by sitting down.* "So, listen: I just wanted to make sure you didn't have any questions about this afternoon."

Harlan shot me a blank look. "This afternoon?"

"Dress rehearsal," I said. "I'll need you to try on the suit and make sure it fits, then get you up to speed on your dialogue."

"Oh." Harlan blinked. "Well, I mean, I didn't actually—"

"Three o'clock in the auditorium—can you make it?"

He shrugged. "Sure, I guess."

"Great," I said. "That's great, Harlan. You're going to be terrific. And there's something else." I turned to Lenny. "I need a virus."

Lenny just stared at me. He'd gone so pale that the only color remaining in his face were the dark circles under his eyes. The muscles in his throat were twitching, his Adam's apple was bobbing up and down, and I wondered if I was going to have to give him mouth-to-mouth in a minute. "Virus?"

"Something that could turn Santa Claus into a raging monster. Some kind of highly contagious infection." I started flipping through the stacks of pages under my arm, looking for the lyrics to the song at the beginning of act 3. "But it has to rhyme with . . . *sleigh*."

"Oh."

"It doesn't absolutely have to, but it would be nice if I didn't have to rewrite the lyrics for that part, you know?" I gave them a smile that I hoped didn't look too desperate. *Rule #4: Never let them see you sweat.* "See, up till now, I never actually said what the virus was, but I'd like to make it as realistic as possible. I figure since it's scientific and you know all this stuff, you could . . ."

I paused. Both Harlan and Lenny were flicking their eyes back and forth like they hadn't heard a word I'd said.

"What are you two gawking at, anyway?"

Harlan looked at Lenny, who was staring down at his

microscope. "Actually, Lenny, why don't you tell Zooey a little bit about what you've been working on here?"

The tips of Lenny's ears turned bright red. I couldn't see the back of his neck from this angle, but I had a feeling it was red too. I'd seen him like this before, whenever I spoke to him directly.

"Well, I, uh . . ." He turned and glanced at the blackboard, which was full of equations that Einstein himself probably would've needed a calculator to figure out.

"Why don't you just take a look for yourself?" Harlan said, nodding at the microscope.

"Oh," I said. "Okay."

"Fair warning," Harlan said. "Be prepared to be amazed."

I crossed my arms and pretended to shiver. "Ooh. Chills."

As I leaned toward the microscope, tucking a strand of hair behind my ear, I heard footsteps in the doorway behind me. When I looked back, I saw Mick Mason walking in with Keegan Hoke and Deke Chambers.

"That's a great idea," Mick said. "Let's all take a peek, huh?"

# FOUR ::: LENNY

I never even saw them come in—Mick, and the two jerks that followed him around like scavengers, bottom-feeders that lived on the random scraps of viciousness that floated in Mick's wake like debris off a garbage scow. Their names were Keegan and Deke, but Harlan called them Sid and Nancy after some punk rockers from the '70s.

Anyway, before I knew it, they were in the lab, Mick in front and the other two hanging back, sauntering over toward us with big, slanting yellow grins on their faces. Sid was actually cracking his knuckles, and Nancy was picking his teeth, as if they were both trying harder than usual to be tough-guy clichés.

I couldn't believe it. For the first time ever, the girl of my dreams—whom I'd literally dreamt about *just last night*—was standing here in the lab, showing visible interest in my groundbreaking discovery, which was destined to shake the foundations of molecular biology to their very core, and Mick Mason had to show up *again* to humiliate me, possibly to death.

"What do *you* want?" Zooey asked. She hadn't looked through the microscope yet, and now I had the sinking feeling that she never would.

"Oh, I dunno," Mick said, looking around at the Bunsen burners and Florence flasks. "This is science class, right?" He walked past a rack of petrie dishes, where one of the biology classes had been cultivating some exotic bacteria. "Maybe I wanna do some *research*."

"Leave those alone," I said.

"What, these?" He picked up one of the petrie dishes, dropped it on the floor, and stepped on it, cracking it under his boot heel. "Whoops."

"Mick . . ." Zooey said.

"That's what you do here, right?" Mick tipped over another petrie dish and shook it, looking slightly disappointed when nothing visible fell out. Then he shot a glance back to Sid, who stepped outside, while the other one, Nancy, closed the door and stationed himself there. "Like, experiments and stuff?"

"Yo, man," Harlan said, moving forward with his chin

up and his shoulders raised, "you heard him. Leave it alone."

Mick turned and looked at Harlan. For a second I expected the usual back-and-forth between them: taunts, threats, jeers, sizing each other up, all the typical grunt-and-bluster that guys go through before one of them either backs down or blows up.

But Mick just punched Harlan in the stomach. I could actually hear the wind go out of Harlan's lungs in a soft whoosh, and he doubled over, clutching his gut and trying to breathe.

"What'd you say?" Mick asked, towering over him. "What'd you just say to me? Huh?"

But Harlan couldn't answer, and neither could I. That frozen feeling had spread across the entire corner of the lab where I was standing.

"Quit it, Mick," Zooey said. "Just leave him alone."

"Oh, I'll leave him alone." He started walking toward Zooey, his long arms swinging casually at his sides. Zooey stood her ground, put her hand on her hip and cocked her head, trying to act casual, but I could tell she wasn't sure what he was going to do either.

"C'mere," Mick said, grabbing her. "Hey, what happened to your sticker? Aren't you nice anymore?"

"Knock it off!"

"Gimme a kiss."

"I said *stop!*"

"Come on, it's Christmas."

Watching all this, I realized there was a pressure rising in my chest, like a balloon expanding somewhere between my stomach and my lungs. It had been building up until I couldn't stand it anymore.

"Let her go," I said.

Mick stopped and swung around to look at me, eyebrows arched, his whole face screwed up as if he couldn't believe his ears. *"What?"*

"You heard me." The words sounded even shakier, more of a mouse's squeak than an actual human voice, but I managed to get them out.

Mick let go of Zooey as if she didn't interest him anymore and walked slowly across the lab toward me. "You just don't get it, do you, Cyrus?" Reaching out with both hands, he gave me the slightest finger tap in the middle of my chest, but it was still enough to move me three steps back. "You're a nobody in this school. You're freakin' invisible."

"Invisible things can still have mass," I mumbled.

His head jerked forward and hung slightly sideways, like a broken jack-in-the-box on a loose spring. "What?"

"In physics." Somewhere over Mick's shoulder, I could see Harlan shaking his head back and forth, making furious slashing gestures across his neck and mouthing the words *No, Lenny, stop.* But I couldn't stop. Something had cracked open inside me now, and it all came babbling out in an anxious, unstoppable flood. "Down on the subatomic level, there's a certain type of elementary particle called a strange quark. It's not one of the more common ones, and it's not even particularly stable—it only exists through high-energy collisions." Mick was still staring at me, his piggy black eyes narrowed and blinking steadily, as if he were waiting for the words to travel down a long and crooked tube to his brain. "But when it meets its antiparticle, which has the same mass but the opposite sign, the two will annihilate each other."

"*Annihilate.*" Mick grinned, back on familiar ground. "I know that word." He walked back over to the counter where my microscope sat. "Like, I'm gonna *annihilate* your experiment."

"No," I said. "Leave that alone!"

"Who's gonna make me?" he said. "You?" The idea seemed to amuse and disgust him at the same time. "You're a strange freakin' quark, all right, Cyrus, I'll give you that." He ran his dirty, long-nailed fingers over the curve of the microscope's arm. "Tell you what: You get down on your knees and beg me and maybe—*maybe*—I'll leave it alone." And then, with another look at me: "Go ahead. Anytime."

He stood there, waiting.

But I didn't beg him.

I just punched him.

:::

Looking back, it was one of those moments that don't feel real, even when they're happening. Mick went stumbling backwards into the counter, arms flailing out to catch himself, and one of his elbows hit the microscope, knocking it sideways and sending it crashing to the floor. Glass splintered. Slides broke. Somewhere on the subatomic level, my microscopic Singer Award–winning nano-rats went scurrying away, lost among the dust particles.

Everything went red. The next thing I knew I was on top of him, swinging, and he was underneath me, calling me a psycho and trying to get free.

I didn't stop until I felt the hand on my shoulder pulling me off and I heard a voice in my ear saying, "Lenny, please, stop, that's enough."

Even in the heat of anger, I realized I knew that voice. It was Zooey.

## FIVE ::: HARLAN

They didn't suspend him.

It was actually weird seeing Lenny's parents and our vice principal, Mr. Cheney, trying to figure out how to discipline the poor kid. The problem had simply never come up before. Sure, Lenny had been to the office before, but always as the victim of somebody else's abuse. This time there wasn't a scratch on him—unless you counted the knuckles of his right hand. Mick Mason, on the other hand, looked like he'd fallen out of the butt-kick tree and hit every branch on the way down. He swore that Lenny had tried to kill him, and from the injuries on his face, people almost believed him.

But then they talked to me, and after I told them what

happened with Mick and Zooey, the school decided to let Lenny go with a warning. It didn't make Lenny feel any better. He'd lost his entire experiment along with the mini-rats, and Dr. Snyder suspended his lab privileges because of what happened to the microscope.

Lenny's parents only made matters worse.

"All they talk about is how this is going to look for *them*," Lenny told me. "You know, how humiliating it is for two Nobel Prize–winning scientists to have a kid who gets kicked out of the middle school science lab— for breaking a microscope. Now they're talking about shipping me off to Brixton Academy next year."

"Again?" I asked. "I thought they were over that." Brixton Academy was an expensive boarding school back east, where geniuses like Lenny studied math and science for twelve hours a day. It was equipped with state-of-the-art lab equipment and staffed by guys who designed rockets for NASA, and generally sounded like a total nightmare. "Did you tell them about the experiment?"

"Are you kidding? My dad's on autopilot. That's the worst part. I mean, I know I'm invisible here at school, but I didn't realize how invisible I was at home until I got in trouble."

"Lenny—"

"They don't even know Zooey's name. I've been talking about her for five years, and they still think her name is Zephyr."

"Have you tried talking to her?"

"I went up to her in the cafeteria at lunch," Lenny said. "I actually got up the nerve to walk over there. She looked at me like I was some kind of psycho."

"Lenny, look—"

"I don't understand," he said. "You think she prefers jerks like Mick Mason to me? You think she actually feels *sorry* for him?"

"Dude, don't be stupid."

"I'm not stupid! I'm the smartest kid in this school!"

"There's different kinds of stupid," I said.

"What's that supposed to mean?"

"Lenny," I said, "you're a genius, okay? Nobody disputes that. But she's a *girl.* You can't apply the properties of physics here."

Lenny didn't answer. I'd never seen him so down. For the rest of the day, he shrank so deeply into himself that it seemed like he'd eventually collapse into a black hole of total depression, another eighth grade casualty.

Meanwhile, I had problems of my own.

"I'm burning up in this thing," I muttered.

"Hold still," Zooey said. "We're almost done."

It was Wednesday, our final dress rehearsal, and we were backstage at the school auditorium while Zooey tugged and plucked at my costume, trying to make it fit. Out on stage I could hear the rest of the cast chattering away—elves and scientists, soldiers and reindeer, along with Mrs. Cassidy, our music teacher, practicing scales on the piano. Aria's voice rose above it all, sharp and bossy, telling everybody to quiet down and take their places for the next musical number. All the while, Zooey kept fussing with my headpiece, and finally, with a sigh, she finished and took a step back.

"Okay, turn around."

I caught my breath. The creature staring back at me from the mirror was a massive, lumpy Santa-beast in a tattered red suit, with a scraggly beard and a huge, pillow-stuffed gut. The foam mask fit over my head like a hood, and I had rubber claws sprouting from the ends of my gloves.

"Holy crap."

"What do you think?"

"How am I supposed to sing in this thing?"

"Just be loud. Don't worry about staying on key. You're supposed to sound scary."

"I can hardly breathe."

"You'll get used to it." She took me by both shoulders and guided me on stage. "Careful. Don't trip on the jack-in-the-box."

The set was a ruined toyshop made to look like the North Pole after some horrific catastrophe. Aria was playing Mrs. Claus—the main female role, naturally—and she was standing in her red sequined gown next to George McDonald, dressed as a broken nutcracker with his jaw gaping open. Hundreds of Styrofoam peanuts lay scattered across the floor to represent snow blown in through broken windows.

"All right," Zooey said, clapping her hands, "places, everybody." The cast got up and moved to their spots. "Act one, scene three. Harlan, hurry up, come *on*." She grabbed me by the belt and swung me around behind the plywood sleigh, shoving me down until I was out of sight. "You remember your cue?"

"Yeah." I was actually more worried about knocking over the canvas flat behind me, but I squatted down behind the sleigh and ducked my head. Drops of sweat were already trickling down my back.

"Okay." Zooey signaled back at Jimmy Colton, who was running the light board. "Places, everybody. Lights?"

I held my breath and got ready.

# SIX ::: ZOOEY

The lights went down, and I felt my scalp prickling in anticipation. Even though it was just a rehearsal, that moment when the auditorium went quiet I could hear my heart pounding in my ears. In those few seconds, I felt like I was playing every part on stage, like I was every actor saying every line that I'd written.

In the silence, I pointed at Tej Singh and Priscilla Shrewsbury, giving them their cue. They stepped out from behind the curtain, dressed in military fatigues, crunching their way through the Styrofoam peanuts.

"Wait a second, Lieutenant," Priscilla said. "Look at this."

"Whoa." Tej shined his flashlight across the darkened stage. "What happened here?"

"I don't know, but it doesn't look good."

"What could do something like this?" Tej asked, looking around. "Polar bears? Wolves?"

"Not this far north," Priscilla said, and I realized that I was mouthing the words along with her. *Rule #1: Know your own story inside and out.* "North Pole security systems are top-notch. Which means somebody disabled them from the inside."

Tej took another step, and I shot a glance over at Harlan in the zombie Santa costume, crouched behind the sleigh. My whole body tensed with anticipation. In about ten seconds, he was supposed to jump up, screaming, and scare Tej and Priscilla to death.

Then everything went wrong.

When Harlan jumped, his right knee caught the sleigh and the whole thing teetered forward. He tried to hold it in place, but his leg was still in the air and he lost his balance, bumping into the canvas set behind him so that the sleigh and the backdrop both fell over with a crash. When the echoes faded, I heard somebody—probably Aria—let out a loud groan of disgust.

"What?" Harlan turned around. "What happened?" Except that he hadn't learned how to enunciate behind the mask and beard, so it came out mushy and muffled. *Muh? Muh appen?*

"It's okay." I clapped my hands. "Bring up the house-lights." The lights came on. "Jerry? Alisa? Can you guys give me a hand here?" I signaled to two elves, and the three of us lifted the fallen sleigh back into place while a couple of volunteer stagehands set the background up-right.

"Hey," Harlan said, and I could tell that he was trying to speak more clearly through the beard, "I'm sorry."

"Don't worry about it."

"You know, maybe I should just run on stage instead of jumping up. I could still scream and everything. That way—"

"It's fine, Harlan. Just be more careful next time. We'll work on your blocking." I caught a glimpse of white underwear in the torn seat of the Santa costume. "Oh—you, uh, ripped your pants."

"What? Where?" He reached around in back, turning away from me. Other kids were drifting over, Aria and Macy Yi and George McDonald, and Harlan backed away, trying to find a quiet corner. "Can you help me take this thing off?"

"Never mind," I said. "We'll fix it later. We need to keep going."

"What am I supposed to do in the meantime?"

"Don't bend over."

"Can I at least take off my mittens?"

"No time," I said. "We're going again in five minutes."

Harlan plunked himself down at the foot of the stage. The houselights had come up and I saw Aria charging across the stage in her full red velvet Mrs. Claus regalia and makeup. She looked like the Ghost of Christmas Gone Berserk.

"What's going on?" she snapped, waving one arm across the stage. "What just happened?"

"Relax," I said. "It was an accident."

"Our first performance is the day after tomorrow!"

I took a breath and tried to stay calm. "Things happen, Aria. Martha Gelhorn-Smith says—"

"Don't you get it?" She was shouting now, and everybody had stopped to listen to her. "You're not some bigtime producer! You're just some geeky eighth grade girl, and your big holiday production is going to be a total disaster." Stepping closer, she lowered her voice. "If I were directing this play, it would have gone like clockwork. No ripped costumes or broken sets. No missed cues. *Clockwork.*"

I felt my throat tighten as a slow burn of embarrassment crept up toward my hairline. I looked over and saw Harlan sitting at the foot of the stage in his Santa costume. At some point during Aria's outburst, Lenny Cyrus had drifted into the gym and was standing next to him. Both of them were watching me, along with the rest of the cast and crew, to see how I was going to handle this near mutiny. *Rule #2: Everybody has a plan until they get hit.*

"I'm sorry you feel that way, Aria," I said. "I hope you realize how much I really appreciate your hard work."

"You *hope?*" Her mouth puckered. "You know, that's the difference between you and me, Zooey. I make things happen, while losers like you sit around and *hope.*" She started to walk away, and turned back and looked at me. "Oh, and by the way, you need to change Harlan's entrance. He's going to kill himself jumping over the sleigh."

"He'll be fine," I said—and hoped it was true.

## SEVEN : : : LENNY

After Zooey walked out of earshot, Harlan turned and looked at me. He was still wearing a zombie Santa mask, and he should have looked scary, but at the moment I was too excited to notice. There was an idea exploding in my head, the biggest one yet, and I couldn't wait another second to get it out.

"So listen," I said. "I started thinking about what you were saying about changing Zooey's mind about me, and it occurred to me: What if I could?"

"Could what?" Harlan asked.

"What if I could *literally* change her mind?"

"What if I *literally* have no idea what you're talking about?"

"Harlan, listen to me." I took in a deep breath. It was vital that he understand exactly how important this was. "We're best friends, right?"

"Yeah."

"And you know how I feel about Zooey."

"Uh, yeah," he said, "pretty clear on that one, thanks."

I stood there next to the stage telling him my idea, and just saying it out loud got me more excited. I mean, this idea was more than beautiful. It was *elegant*. My dad always says that a truly elegant idea is one that solves multiple complex problems with one simple solution, so I knew he'd be proud of me for this one, even though I could never tell him about it. At least until afterward, when I won the Singer Prize and people started writing books about me, and then reporters and TV people would come to my house and interview my parents, and my dad would say, yes, he always knew that I was a genius, but he never dreamed that I would come up with something so completely incredible at age thirteen.

"Forget it, man," Harlan said. "That's the stupidest idea you've ever had."

I stared at him. "You're joking, right?"

"Do I look like I'm joking?"

"No," I said, "you look like Santa's evil twin."

He tugged at the beard strapped to his face, but it wouldn't come loose. "Seriously, Lenny, trust me. Don't do this. It's not just a terrible idea—it's dangerous."

"What's wrong with it?"

"Only about a million things. What if you hurt her? What if you hurt yourself? What if you can't get back out again?"

"It's one hundred percent scientifically viable. I know exactly what I'm doing. You saw the rats."

"And look what happened to them," he said. "I mean, have you even thought this through? What are you going to tell your parents?"

"That's the beauty of it." The details were popping into my head. "I have independent study for the whole day on Friday. I'll be done by two thirty, three at the latest. It'll be like nothing happened."

"Wait a second," Harlan said, and tried to stand up, but in his zombie Santa costume he couldn't bend his knees to push himself upright, so he just settled for scuttling away on his butt, trying to put as much distance between us as possible. "Why are you involving *me?*"

"Why do you think I'm telling you any of this? I need your help."

"No way."

I sighed. Harlan can be extremely shortsighted sometimes, which is understandable in someone of limited intelligence, but I thought he knew me better than this. "I can't do it without you."

"Then I guess you're not doing it."

"Harlan," Zooey said, "are you ready to go again?"

Harlan and I both looked up and saw her standing

over us. She had her hands on her hips and a little concerned wrinkle between her eyebrows. At this distance I
could smell her. She smelled like vanilla and cinnamon
and lip balm, and her hair looked licorice black, shiny,
sweeping sideways across her forehead. Even her black
glasses made me want to stand up and kiss the tip of
her nose where the last three freckles sat like three tiny
explorers at the end of the universe. All at once I tried to
talk, but my tongue felt as if it had swelled up inside my
mouth like a sponge.

"I was . . . we were . . ." Harlan glanced at me, then
back up at her. "Forget it."

"Lenny, did you think of anything yet?"

I blinked at her. "What?"

"The name of a virus that could turn Santa Claus into
*that*." She pointed at me. "Any ideas?"

I cleared my throat, realized that I was wringing my
hands, and forced myself to stop. "Well." My voice came
out high and squeaky, and I tried again. "I mean, uh—
you know, actually . . . there was an interesting article in
last month's *Scientific American* about a . . . neurological
virus."

"Oh really? What was it called?"

My mind went blank. I *knew* the name of the virus. I'd
memorized it without even meaning to, because that's
what happens when you've got a photographic memory: your brain just accumulates this stuff like dust bun-
nies under the bed—the electrochemical properties of

carbon nanotubes and classifications of dark matter. But at the moment all I could think of was that Zooey's eyes looked like shiny black marbles, and how she had perfect skin, like the skin of a peach.

"Lenny?" she prompted. "Hello?"

"Sorry. I don't . . . I mean . . ."

Zooey grunted and shook her head. "Keep at it, Genius Boy. Come on, Harlan, break's over. Back to work." She turned to Harlan, stupid Harlan in his stupid zombie Santa outfit, and took hold of his arm, *actually holding his hand* as they walked back to meet with the rest of the cast.

I jumped up on stage next to him, whispering in his ear.

"Harlan," I said, quiet enough so Zooey couldn't hear, "if you've ever believed in me about anything, believe in this. The idea will work."

"Forget it. No way."

"It's a perfect idea! Nothing's going to go wrong!"

He waved me off with one hand. "That's what you said about the groundhogs in my uncle's camper, and look what happened to them."

"I'm doing this with or without you."

He stopped. "Lenny—"

"You know I will. Help if you want to, but if you don't, then just stay out of the way." I locked eyes with him so he could see how serious I was. "I mean it, Harlan."

He cocked his head, looking ridiculous in the Santa hat and beard. "You're a lousy friend, you know that?"

"No, I'm not." I poked him in his big stuffed belly. "I make your life interesting. Without me you'd just be another kid in an Angry Birds shirt, going to baseball games and eating pizza."

"That sounds pretty good to me."

"Hey," I said, "anytime you want to get off the Lenny Express . . ."

"How about right now?"

"Fine," I said. "I'll do it by myself." I turned and started walking away. I got five steps before I heard him behind me.

"Lenny?"

I stopped, looking back. "What?"

"You're seriously going through with this with or without me?"

"Absolutely."

Harlan stood there in the zombie Santa suit. I could feel the frustration coming off of him in waves. "You're a real jackwagon sometimes, you know that?"

"Does that mean you're in?"

"What choice do I have?" Harlan asked. "Somebody has to keep you from killing yourself . . ." He glanced back in the direction where Zooey had gone. "Or her."

# EIGHT ::: HARLAN

On Friday morning I found Lenny in the science lab before first period, hovering over a big cardboard box of equipment.

"What took you so long?"

"Nice to see you too." I dropped my backpack. My *Escape Claus* script was sticking out of the top. "It's seven forty-five in the morning," I said. "That's when you told me to—"

"Whatever, let's get started. Close the door. We don't have much time." He peeled off his T-shirt and started unbuckling his jeans, pushing them down over his hips.

"Whoa," I said. "What do you think you're doing?"

"Getting ready." He kicked off his shoes and peeled off his socks so that he was standing there in his tightie-whities, took out a beaker of some kind of sticky goo, and started smearing it all over his chest. It smelled like eucalyptus mixed with petroleum jelly.

"What is that stuff?"

"It's the guanosine sheath." He turned around, giving me a view of his scrawny shoulder blades. "Rub some on my back, will you?"

"What's in it?"

"It's a superconductive purine nucleoside ointment comprising guanine attached to a—"

"Okay, sorry I asked." I scooped out some of the guanine and started smearing it down his spine. "Ugh, it's tingly. This stuff isn't radioactive, is it?"

"No, it's perfectly stable."

"So why are you—"

"It's going to protect me in case I get a hole in this." Lenny turned, reached into the cardboard box by his feet, and pulled out a black neoprene wetsuit. He started slipping it on. "Hand me that oxygen tank, will you?"

I lifted the tank and helped him strap it over his shoulders. "How long will this last?"

"Sixty minutes. Which should be plenty of time."

"Wait—I thought you were going to need six hours."

"I've rigged the regulator to draw oxygen directly from the hemoglobin in the bloodstream. The tank is just a backup. I shouldn't need it at all."

"What if it doesn't work?"

"It's going to work, Harlan, okay? Do me a favor and at least try to be supportive for once, all right?"

I stood by while he put on the flippers and face mask, attaching the halogen headlamp and switching it on so that it threw an intense white glare across the lab. Then he reached up for a radio headset lying on the counter next to a flat slab of homemade electronics that I hadn't noticed until now.

"What's that thing?"

"This, my friend, is where the magic happens." He gestured proudly at it. "Meet the nanodeck."

It was a heavy-looking black rectangle about the size of a shoebox, bristling with dozens of exposed copper wires and vacuum tubes. A thick orange electrical cord snaked from the back and ended at the outlet next to

the sink. Lenny switched it on and the whole thing began vibrating slightly. A red button on the top started blinking on and off.

"Okay, look." He settled the headset over his ears. "I've patched myself in to your phone. If I call, it's an emergency, which means you'd better answer. You need to keep your phone on. Don't let it go straight to voice mail."

"Sure thing, boss."

"I mean it, Harlan. I don't know exactly what's going to happen in there."

"Wait, I thought you told me—"

"Just make sure you pick up if I call you."

A terrible possibility occurred to me. "What if I'm on stage? It's opening night!"

"I'll be done by two. The play doesn't start until three thirty, right?"

"Yeah," I said, "I guess, but—"

"Okay, listen," Lenny said. "I came up with a code word—a way of letting you know when I've reached my final destination." He handed me a slip of paper with a single word written on it.

"*Chromoblastomycosis?*" I stared at him. "Can't it just be, like, *safe?*"

"No." Lenny shook his head. "It has to be something you'd never hear otherwise, so you know it's me saying it and not Zooey."

"Wait," I said. "You're going to be talking to me through her mouth?"

"I'm not sure how it's going to work, Harlan. I've never done this before, okay?"

"Yeah, well, that doesn't exactly inspire a boatload of confidence."

"Trust me." He held out his hand. In his palm were two tiny halves of an empty gelatin capsule. I looked at them.

"What used to be in there?"

"Vitamin C. You know what to do, right?"

"I guess so."

"Then I'll see you in six hours."

"Wait! How are you going to know when the time's up?"

"I built a digital timer into the mask."

"You never told me what happens after six hours."

"What do you think?" He gave me an impatient glare. "The process wears off."

"Wait, you didn't tell me how—"

"Stand back, Harlan," he said, and hit the switch.

A wave of red light burst out of the black machine, bathing the room in a flash and temporarily blinding me.

And Lenny disappeared.

I stared at the empty space on the floor of the lab where he'd been standing just a second earlier. I found myself looking around the room, as if I somehow expected him to pop up from behind one of the counters.

Then my phone rang, playing, "She Blinded Me with Science." I fumbled it out of my backpack. "Hello?"

"Dude," Lenny's voice said, "hurry up with the empty capsule."

I took another look in every direction, feeling totally stupid. "Where are you?"

"I'm right here in front of you," he snapped. "But I'm still shrinking. Come on, let's go, before I'm so small you can't see me at all."

"How small are you now?" I stared down at the floor, moving my head back and forth like a kid who'd lost a pocketful of change. "I can't even see you now."

"Get down on the floor. Carefully."

I crouched down, fixing my eyes more closely on the gray squares of worn-out linoleum. "I still can't—"

"Lower."

I got down on my hands and knees and pressed my cheek to the floor until I could actually smell the disinfectant that they'd used the night before. "Where . . . ?"

"Get the capsule," Lenny's voice barked in the phone, sounding full-size in my ear. Apparently shrinking down to the subatomic level hadn't made him any less bossy. "Set it down on the floor next to me."

I laid the two halves of the open capsule on the linoleum, hoping I'd at least gotten it close. There was dust under the radiator and pencils that kids had dropped, a nickel and some brown crumbs of something in the corner, but I couldn't see him at all.

"Harlan?" a voice said behind me.

I jumped and turned around, scooping up the capsule. Zooey was walking into the science lab. She had her usual morning Diet Coke in one hand and the front page of the newspaper in the other.

She pushed her glasses up and gave me one of those little Zooey frowns, the kind that looked half puzzled and half amused. "What were you doing on the floor?"

"Oh, I just—I lost a contact lens."

"I didn't know you wore contacts."

"Oh, yeah, I mean, I just started. It popped right out, and—"

"Here." She put her books on the counter and started walking toward me. "I'll help you look."

"That's okay." I glanced down at the capsule in my hand, hoping that I'd given Lenny enough time to get inside, and slipped the two halves of it together. "What . . . I mean, how come you're here so early?"

"It's opening day—afternoon, whatever. Are you nervous?"

"Me?" I shook my head. "No. Not at all."

"Good," she said, "because I think this afternoon's going to be great. I've got a few ideas for your entrance. Did you see the paper?"

She unfolded the front page and showed it to me. The headline read:

# WRECK THE HALLS
## CMS Students Plan Their "Escape" in Holiday Horror Musical

Underneath was a long article with a big picture of me on stage in my zombie Santa suit, with Tej and Priscilla dressed as soldiers, and Aria in her Mrs. Claus costume, while Zooey stood by giving us direction.

"It's online, too," Zooey said. "With full-color photos. And supposedly there's a TV crew from WCRW arriving sometime before lunch."

"Wow." I managed a smile. "You're famous."

"Don't tell Aria that," Zooey said, and rolled her eyes. "She already thinks she belongs on the A-list for life. Anyway"—she handed me the newspaper clipping—"I wanted you to have that one. My mom's got a whole stack of them at home. She's threatening to send out a new batch of Christmas cards just so she can put the article in there."

"Thanks," I said.

"No problem." She took a step back and glanced around the lab. "No Lenny this morning?"

"He's . . . ah . . ." I tried not to look down at the vitamin capsule getting warm in my palm. All at once the collar of my sweater felt extra tight and itchy. "Man, I'm really thirsty." I glanced at her Diet Coke. "You mind?" When she frowned at me, I smiled. "I won't backwash, I swear."

"Sure, I guess." She handed me the bottle and I took a sip, then casually dropped the tiny gelatin capsule into the bottle before I put the cap back on it.

"Thanks," I said, "that hits the spot. I just get this weird craving for aspartame sometimes. Must be my ADD or something."

She smiled. "How's your stomach?"

"My stomach?"

"Where Mick punched you?"

"Oh," I said, "I'm fine. I just got the wind knocked out of me, that's all."

"He's such a jerk."

"Yeah," I said. "But that was great what Lenny did, wasn't it? I mean, he really stood up for you."

"Stood up for his microscope, you mean," Zooey said. "That's what really got him angry, when that thing got broken and ruined his experiment."

"That's not true," I said, "he didn't like the way Mick was treating you."

"Whatever." She took a drink of Diet Coke. "Well, I should get to class. I'll see you for fourth period."

I nodded. She and I both had gym fourth period, and we always walked over there together. It was just a casual kind of thing that always made Lenny jealous. Neither of us planned it, but he always complained that he never got a chance to get that close to her.

Well, he was close to her now, wasn't he?

Zooey gathered her notebooks and started toward the door when my phone started playing "She Blinded Me with Science." I looked down at the display and saw Lenny's name on the screen and hit Talk. "Hello?"

"*Harlan?*"

It was Lenny. He was shouting, but I could barely hear him. The connection was full of background noise,

loud whooshing and splashing and growling that dis-
torted through the earpiece. It sounded like he was calling from inside an active volcano. "Can you hear me?"

"Yeah," I said. "Barely."

"I'm in!"

"You're . . . in?" I glanced up and saw that Zooey had
stopped and turned around in the doorway and was
gazing at me. I flicked my eyes down at her stomach.
"You mean, like, *in* in?" I lowered my voice, cupping my
hand over the phone. "What . . . what's it like?"

"I'm not sure yet. It's really dark, and something happened to my headlamp when I landed. I'm still trying to
fix it."

"Is that Lenny?" Zooey asked. "Where is he?"

I lowered the cell and covered the mouthpiece. "He's,
uh, nearby."

"Can I talk to him?"

"You want to . . . ?" I brought the phone back to my
mouth. "Hey, Lenny, ah . . . Zooey wants to talk to you."

"*What?* No, I can't—not right now."

"Why not?"

The background noise got louder, and the last thing I
heard was a scream.

# NINE ::: ZOOEY

I walked out of the science lab, my thoughts still tangled up between this afternoon's performance and what Harlan had said about Lenny standing up for me back in the lab. I'd never seen Lenny get that angry before. The broken microscope had to fit into the equation somewhere, and his experiment—whatever it was—was probably a lot more important to him than protecting me from Mick Mason.

Suddenly something slammed into me from behind, hard enough to knock me off my feet.

"*Ow!*" I dropped my notebook and Diet Coke, my hands flying out to break my fall, and I turned around and looked up to see Mick Mason's two best buddies, Keegan Hoke and Deke Chambers, grappling with each other against a bank of lockers. "Why don't you two baboons watch where you're going?"

"Sorry." Keegan grinned. "Lover-boy here thinks it's Valentine's Day."

"Yeah, right," Deke said. "You're the one who jumped me."

"You wish." Keegan took a step toward me, breathing hard. "Here's your notebook or whatever." He was still grinning, his wide face flushed with exertion, his T-shirt wrinkled around the collar where Deke had grabbed him. "And your soda. Since, you know, you dropped it."

"Thanks," I said, taking the bottle back. "You didn't spit in it, did you?"

Keegan looked offended. "Like we'd do that."

I opened the Diet Coke slowly in case it fizzed up everywhere, but it didn't. Oddly, the soda suddenly felt a lot colder than before I dropped it, almost like it was a different bottle, but I didn't give it much thought. I just wanted to get away from Deke and Keegan as quickly as possible.

The auditorium was on the way back to Mr. Early's English class, and even though the first-period bell was about to ring, I couldn't help sticking my head in there on the way by. Mr. Early knew how important *Escape Claus* was to me—he was the first person that I showed the play to last year—and over the past couple of weeks, he'd sometimes let me work on revisions in class, so I wasn't worried about showing up a few minute late.

I pushed open the door to the auditorium and stuck my head inside, smelling the familiar combination of floor polish mixed with paint and plaster from the sets. There were about thirty sleepy-looking kids standing around inside in sneakers, shorts, and T-shirts, waiting for our PE teacher, Mr. Shoenwald, to come out of his office and start yelling at them to do pushups.

Trying not to draw attention to myself, I slipped around the edge of the gym and climbed the steps onto the stage, hoping for an idea about how I could fix Harlan's big entrance. *Rule #6: Inspiration comes when you least expect it.*

The curtains were closed over the North Pole set that I'd spent the last three months building, and I ducked beneath them. Since the end of September, this place had become as familiar to me as my own house, and I knew every step of it, every sticky pulley and squeaky floorboard. All the Styrofoam peanuts had been carefully swept and bagged in preparation for our very first show.

That was when I heard them—voices murmuring quietly in the dark, on the other side of the set.

I stopped and cocked my head, listening. One of voices was Aria's, and that was already weird, because she had never spoken quietly in her life. It sounded as if she was standing on the opposite side of the canvas backdrop, but with the stage's acoustics, I could hear every word.

"Did you get it?" she whispered.

"It's already taken care of," a boy's voice answered.

"You're sure?"

"I promised I would, didn't I?"

I took another step and peered through a hole in the canvas. It took a minute for my brain to process what my eyes were seeing. Aria was standing at the back of the stage, still wearing her coat. The boy in front of her was Mick Mason. He was wearing his usual beat-up old leather jacket with buckles hanging off it, holding something that I couldn't see.

My thoughts spun back to earlier that morning. I had passed Mick in the hallway about twenty minutes earlier, on my way into the science lab, but what was he doing here in my home turf? He had his hand up by Aria's face and was kind of running his fingers through her hair, and shockingly, she didn't seem to mind. In fact, she seemed to be enjoying it.

I just stood there, frozen in total disbelief. Mick Mason and Aria Keen? Had the universe just flipped itself completely inside out?

If so, that wasn't the only thing twisting upside down. As I stood here watching them, my stomach was getting that twitchy, fluttering feeling that felt a little like hunger but definitely wasn't. Was it just opening-day jitters? Martha Gelhorn-Smith calls this the *shpilkes,* which is Yiddish for "nerves." She says she always gets them before she starts a new production, and if they happen to her, then I guess it was okay for them to happen to me.

Meanwhile I kept standing there, watching Mick and Aria.

"You're evil," Aria said, and let out a little chuckle.

"Whatever," Mick said, "it was your idea," but he was smiling too, still touching her hair. He leaned toward her, and for one sickening second I thought they were going to kiss, which, in my current queasy condition, was something I definitely didn't need to see. I took a step backwards, and my foot creaked against a loose floorboard.

"What was that?" Mick stopped and looked straight in my direction. "Who's there?"

I jerked back from my side of the canvas backdrop. Aria turned and looked over too, and I could already hear Mick's big boots thudding around the corner. There was no way that I was going to get out of there before they saw me.

"Zooey?" Aria said. "What are you doing here?"

"I was just checking the sets," I said. "Oh, hey, Mick." I thought I sounded pretty casual, but Mick didn't look convinced. Even in the dim light from under the curtain, I could see him blushing hard, whole constellations of pimples rising over his face and neck like a heat rash.

"How long have you been spying on us?" he said.

"I wasn't spying," I said. "I just got here." And just then, the sick feeling in my stomach got about three times worse, and I realized it wasn't just opening-day jitters.

There was definitely something bad going on in my stomach.

Maybe it was something I ate.

# TEN ::: LENNY

Depending on what Zooey'd had for breakfast, I calculated that I had five minutes tops before the gelatin capsule dissolved completely. After that, I'd be at the mercy of the digestive acids in her stomach.

It turned out that I was about four and a half minutes off.

The ride down had been a jolting, spinning nightmare. Back in the biology lab, Harlan had left the gelatin capsule open so that I could crawl inside before he dropped it in her Diet Coke. When she'd finally tipped back the bottle for a drink, I'd braced myself for impact, though I still wasn't ready when the back of my head slammed into the sticky, vitamin-smelling gelatin coating that lined inside the capsule. Right away, the halogen headlamp cracked and blinked out. Thanks a lot, L.L.Bean.

Now I was down in total darkness, groping around for something to hold on to, and the world exploded with a deafening mixture of growls and splashing noises, followed by a steady hissing sound from outside, like somebody trying to fry an entire pack of bacon. That would be the acids eating through the gelatin. Somehow I managed to activate the hands-free phone I'd installed in the dive mask and initiate a shouted conversation with Harlan to let him know I'd gotten down in one piece, more or less. I could hardly hear him talking. Not surprising, since I already felt like I'd gone over Niagara Falls and landed in the middle of a category 5 hurricane. Everything was a lot warmer in here and more humid, and right away my goggles fogged up on my face.

". . . Lenny?" Harlan's voice crackled from the headpiece, and then it was gone.

I started to answer, and out of nowhere, sizzling pain hit my arm like a splash of hot grease, burning right through the wetsuit. I screamed and shot both hands out instinctively in front of me, scrambling up through the darkness along what felt like a slippery, uneven wall.

That was when my headlamp came back on.

For a second I just stood there, unable to speak, think, or even breathe. I was perched along the edge of a rippled cliff above a dark ocean of Diet Coke, fizzing and sloshing around. Down below, chunks of partially digested breakfast cereal—it looked like Lucky Charms, blue stars and green clovers—were floating around in the soda like debris from a colorful Irish shipwreck. My first thought was *Wow, Zooey Andrews eats an even unhealthier breakfast than I do.*

Turning back, I looked up along the slippery walls rising up around me on all sides. I don't know what I was expecting, but from here the inside of Zooey's stomach looked like a teenage girl's bedroom, thirty different shades of pink coming at me from every imaginable direction while I fought to get my equilibrium. Somewhere down below, the very last of the gelatin capsule was dissolving like a leaky rowboat, sinking beneath artificially sweetened waves.

"You there," a voice growled from up above, close enough that I almost lost my balance, "where's your pass?"

"Wait," I said. "You can *talk?*"

"Of course we can talk."

I tilted back my head and stared up along the stomach wall, trying to take in the torrent of activity above. Colonies of giant gray and yellow rod-shaped bacteria were squirming in every direction, but one of them— a long, semitransparent jelly-bean-looking thing with a flagellum whipping back and forth—wasn't going anywhere, just staring at me with a pair of enormous blank, sightless eyes. It looked annoyed just to see me here.

"I was just . . ." My own voice sounded small and hollow, lost inside the giant space. "I just landed here."

The thing whacked me with its whip-tail. "That's not an answer. You're not authorized to be here. Where's your digestive pass?"

"I don't have one."

The whip-tail lashed out again wildly, missing me completely, and I realized the bacteria couldn't really see me at all. What I'd thought were its eyes were probably just partially extruded organelles.

I stared at the thing and tried to classify it based on what I remembered from microanatomy, but without the proper lab equipment, it was impossible to confirm a valid identification. Dr. Snyder always said that for as long as we've been studying the normal flora of the human gut, scientists actually don't know much about it. It's a whole microscopic cityscape of unclassified bugs down here, a lot of which help keep things in balance, but the best known—E. coli and H. pylori—are the nasty ones that get out of control and cause real troubles. The rest of them, like the bacteria in front of me now, worked like a digestive sanitation department, maintaining order and pH balance, twenty-four hours a day.

"What's your classification?" it demanded.

"Um," I said, "six?"

"*That's not an answer!*"

"I'm . . . ah . . ." My brain skipped ahead, plucking an answer out of thin air. "*Lactobacillus acidophilus?*"

"Probiotic?"

"Uh, yeah."

"Great," the bacteria muttered. "We're not back on yogurt again, are we? I didn't hear anything about that from upstairs."

"No, sir," I said. "I'm just a supplement. I came down in a tablet with the Diet Coke, and—"

"All right, acidophilus, I didn't ask for your life story. Finish your business and get back to work."

"Yes, sir."

The bacteria was about to turn away, trying to force its way through the mobs of organisms slithering around the walls of the stomach, when it suddenly stopped. In fact, I realized that the entire colony of bacteria had stopped moving for an instant, and then I saw them ripple together in one simultaneous wave, as if a current of heightened awareness was passing over them all at once.

When it turned back toward me, its voice sounded different, darker, more threatening.

"Hold it."

I should've run, or at least made a jump for it. Not that I knew which direction to turn, or could've gone anywhere quickly with the flippers still on my feet. And if I slipped and fell back into the Diet Coke and digestive juices below, Zooey's enzymes would eat through my neoprene suit and the guanosine layer underneath it before I even got a chance to scream.

"We're getting reports of unknown, newly arrived viral activity in this sector," the bacteria said, leaning in. "*You* wouldn't know anything about that, would you?"

"No," I said, "I—"

"Don't move."

They lunged at me. Jerking back on instinct, I felt the pink stomach wall against my back, and at the same second something grabbed my shoulders and yanked me backwards with a slippery pop. Warm, moist tissue pressed in from all sides, suffocating me, and I barely managed to get the mouthpiece and diving regulator into my mouth in time to suck in a breath of oxygen. I couldn't tell if I was being pulled backwards, upward, sideways, or down, but for the moment it didn't seem to matter. All I knew was that I was moving, fast.

"Stay close, bro," a new voice said. "It's gonna get sticky."

I tried to pull back but couldn't get any traction. Out of nowhere, mucous epithelium cells were jostling and shoving past me like elbows and shoulders and overstuffed backpacks—being down here was already more like navigating the hallway between classes than I'd ever expected—and I still couldn't see whatever it was that had rescued me from the bacteria. Rising up in the background I heard a huge roar, like a massive waterfall getting louder by the second.

"Hold on tight," the voice shouted.

"Wait a second—what are you doing?" I craned my

neck and got a quick glimpse of something blue and star-shaped that had glued itself to my shoulders. "Where are we—"

WHOOOSH! Up ahead, a deafening roar of turbulence overtook my words and thoughts at the same time. I had a fraction of a second to process what was about to happen as the thing attached to my wetsuit yanked me forward toward a gushing torrent of dark arterial red.

Then we hit it.

Assuming a resting pulse of seventy-two beats per minute, the average velocity of blood in the human circulatory system is approximately ninety-six cubic centimeters per second. That doesn't sound too bad until you factor in my relative size, which was something like a thousandth of a centimeter—small enough that everything around me was just a wild blur blasting past so fast that I couldn't process any of it.

"Whooo!" the thing on my back shrieked, and I couldn't tell if it was screaming or laughing hysterically as we spiraled around in crazy seasick circles, bumping and thumping off the vessel walls, flying around the twists and turns and shooting through the straightaways at roughly the speed of light. "This is it, baby! Iliac bifurcation! *Feel the rush!*"

I was screaming too—and I *knew* why. I was convinced that I was going to die right here in the bloodstream of the girl I'd been in love with since third grade.

If I didn't drown in her corpuscles, I'd be knocked sense-less against the interior of her arteries. The scuba regu-lator fell from my mouth and I hoped—prayed—that the modifications that I'd made to the diving mask, to draw oxygen directly from Zooey's hemoglobin, would work the way I'd planned. Otherwise this was going to be a *very* short trip.

I sucked in a breath and felt my head spinning as freshly decocted oxygen siphoned through my system, pushing back the noose of blackness that had started tightening around the corners of my vision. Delayed panic jerked up in my throat and I was suddenly sure that I was going to burst into hysterical tears. The thing behind me must have noticed, because it sounded wor-ried.

"Okay, okay," it said, "hey, it's all right, dude. Calm down, huh?"

I looked around and realized we had slowed down, eddying in slower circles and coming to a stop so that my thoughts could catch up with me.

"You all right, man? You aren't gonna, like, spew pro-teins or anything, are you?"

I looked at the thing that had come loose from my back and was now floating in front of me. It was a star-shaped, semiamorphous blob with hundreds of tiny re-ceptors studding its limbs, rippling gently in the capil-lary tidewaters.

"You . . ." I managed. "You're an astrovirus?"

"Hey, bro, watch the labels," the thing snapped, then paused. "I mean, okay, technically you're right." It hesitated. "What are you?"

"Lactobacillus—"

"Aw, come off it," the thing said, waving one tendril dismissively. "You're a virus like me. Takes one to know one, right?" One of the tendrils reached out and brushed against the sleeve of my wetsuit, taking in the whole package—mask, flippers, $O_2$ tank—in one move. "Haven't seen you around before, though. You some kind of new mutation?"

"I guess you could say that."

"What do they call you?"

"Uh . . . L. Cyrus . . . virus."

"The El Cyrus virus?" The thing made a shrugging gesture. "Hey, whatever. I guess you're new to the system, huh? Don't worry, I'll show you around. You dig the stream?"

"Not really."

"Trust me, you will. Especially when you need to get away fast—which you frequently will if you value your life when the NK cells show up." He paused in thought, a process that seemed to require physical effort. "Whatever you do, steer clear of the heart. It's nothing but trouble." It swirled around me a half-dozen times, settling back in front of my face. "Oh, and don't trust Whitey."

"Whitey?"

"White blood cells." The virus nodded grimly. "Those

self-righteous pus-bags are complete jerks. Always blab-bing about the greater good. Big fish in a small pond. They can't touch us, though. Not like the NK. Freaking killing machines, those things." It shuddered. "You see those dudes coming, don't even bother to run." Then it brightened. "But hey, you keep your head down, stick to the stream, and keep moving, they won't even know you're there."

"Where are we now?" I asked.

"Now? Shoot, I dunno. Some backwater capillary bed somewhere. Why? You got somewhere you need to be?"

"As a matter of fact," I said, "yes. I need to get to the brain."

# ELEVEN ::: HARLAN

I was in Mrs. Frank's third-period literature class, trying to think of something intelligent to say about *The Red Badge of Courage,* when the intercom clicked on overhead and the voice of Mr. Cheney, our esteemed vice principal, came through the speaker. The PA made him sound nasal and metallic, like Darth Vader with a chronic sinus infection.

"Mrs. Frank, will you send Harlan Williams to the office, please?"

"He's on his way." Mrs. Frank—a tough old bird probably two years from retirement, who claimed to have spent her formative years following a band called the

Grateful Dead—didn't even glance up from the board. "Hit the bricks, Mr. Williams."

I pushed back my chair and stood up. Of course, everybody turned and looked at me. They all knew about the fight in the lab, and I heard a few people whispering as I walked out the door and down the hall.

I wondered what this was about. As far as I knew, everything had been settled with Mick, and even if it hadn't, none of it was my fault. My biggest role in the whole thing had been getting punched in the gut. I'd just been in the wrong place at the wrong time.

It turned out that was only the beginning of it.

Right away, when I walked into Mr. Cheney's office and saw Lenny's mom and dad sitting there opposite Mr. Cheney, I knew it was bad. All three of them looked up and stared at me.

"Oh, hey, Dr. Cyrus," I said to Lenny's mom, trying to sound casual, as if this sort of thing happened all the time, and then turned to his dad. "Hey . . . Dr. Cyrus." Lenny had told me a long time ago that his parents hated being called Mr. and Mrs., which I guess made sense when you thought about how much time they'd poured into getting multiple doctorates and advanced degrees. I'd been calling them both "doctor" as long as I could remember. It only sounded weird when you said it together, but it was still better than calling them Don and Susan—especially when they both looked like they were prepared to hang me upside down by my toenails.

"Harlan," Mr. Cheney said, "sit down, please."

"Sure, okay." I pulled up the last chair in the office. "What's up?"

"Actually, Harlan," Mr. Cheney said, "we were hoping you might tell us."

I gave them my best confused and innocent look. "Sorry?"

"Mrs. Cyrus called my office this morning," he began, and I saw Lenny's mom wince a little at the way he referred to her, "looking for her son. It seems that Lenny forgot his lunch today, and she was worried that he might go hungry."

"Oh, man," I muttered under my breath. "Lenny, you idiot."

"Excuse me?"

"Nothing, sir." Of all the people I knew, only Lenny could successfully use cutting-edge nanotechnology to insert himself into the human bloodstream and then tip everybody off by forgetting to pack a lunch. "I just—can't believe he'd be that absent-minded, is all."

"That's hardly the point, Mr. Williams. Because as it turns out, Lenny isn't here at all. In fact . . . nobody has seen him all morning." I glanced at Lenny's mom and dad again. "His parents are understandably concerned."

"I wouldn't be surprised if this had something to do with what happened yesterday," Lenny's mother said.

"What about that other boy that was bullying him—that Mick Mason?" She glared at Cheney. "What if he's done something to Lenny?"

"Mrs. Cyrus—"

"*Dr.* Cyrus," she corrected him, and turned back to me. "Harlan, I want you to answer me honestly. Have you seen my son?"

"I'm sorry," I said, "but I really don't—"

Just then my phone started ringing—"She Blinded Me with Science"—while the screen began flashing Lenny's name. His parents knew that ringtone: they'd picked it out for him. Some kind of eighties joke that they thought was hilarious, no doubt, but now it didn't seem funny at all.

"I think you'd better answer that," Lenny's mom said.

I brought the phone up to my ear. "Hello?"

"*Harlan?*" Lenny shouted. In the background, a steady roar blasted through the receiver, distorting into big sizzling blurts of static that sounded like somebody dropping radioactive waste from five stories into a giant vat of pudding. "Are you there?"

"Yeah," I said, "except . . ." I lowered my voice to a whisper. "Dude, your parents are here."

"You gotta talk louder. I can't hear you!"

Lenny's mom was glaring at me. "Put him on speakerphone."

"I really don't think—" I started.

"Now, please, Harlan."

I hit the speakerphone button and a surge of white noise roared through the tiny speaker. "Harlan!" Now Lenny sounded like he was calling from inside a wind tunnel. "You're not going to believe where I am!"

Lenny's dad stood up. "And where is that, son?"

There was nothing from Lenny for a long moment. "Wait—*Dad?*" Lenny's voice got quieter, but just a little. "Harlan, is my *dad* with you?"

"I tried to warn you," I said.

"We're both here," his mom cut in. "The question is, Leonard, where are you?"

"Hang on just a second—" All of a sudden there was a huge upsurge of noise, rising and curling like a tidal wave slamming into the beach, and at the very peak of it we all heard Lenny let out a long howl—"*whhhoooOOOAAAHH —AIIIIGGGGHHH—OOOOOO!!!*"—except this time the howl broke off into what sounded like wild, shrieking laughter. If I hadn't known better, I would've thought he was at our indoor water park, TsunamiLand, or surfing killer waves on a boogie board.

"Oh my goodness—Lenny?" Lenny's mom turned to her husband. "What on earth has gotten into him?" She stood up and crossed the office, grabbed my phone, and held it in both hands. "Lenny, it's your mother. Can you hear me? Where are you?"

"Mom? I'm okay—" Now he was panting, sounding out of breath but happier than I'd heard him in a long time. "It's all right, I'm fine."

"I—I don't understand." She looked back to Lenny's dad. "Is he *laughing?*"

"Leonard Albert Cyrus," his dad said, rising up out of his chair. He was a tall man with a deep voice, and until you heard him use it, you forgot how scary he could be. "You listen to me. You tell me where you are, right now, do you understand? And I mean *right now*. Or you are going to wish you'd never gotten out of bed today, young man. Do I make myself perfectly clear?"

"Dad . . ." Lenny said, still sounding like he was catching his breath, "you remember the Von Friedrich experiment?"

"Von Friedrich," Dr. Cyrus repeated. "Right, of course I do, but I fail to see—"

"I made it work."

Dr. Cyrus pursed his lips and scowled. "That's impossible."

"No, it's not," Lenny said. "Listen to this." All at once we heard a faint gurgling noise followed by a series of high-pitched metallic pings like submarine sonar. "You hear that? Those are axons and dendrites. Purkinje cells undergoing auto-induced electrochemical stimulation."

"I'm sorry," Mr. Cheney said. "What is he talking about?"

"That's . . ." Lenny's dad closed his mouth, frowned, then shot a glance at Cheney's desk. "Give me a piece of paper."

Mr. Cheney scowled. "What?"

Lenny's dad snatched a yellow legal pad and a pencil from under Cheney's nose, knocking over a pen and pencil caddy in the process, along with Cheney's 2003 Principal of the District award. The pens and pencils spilled all over the desk and went rolling onto the floor.

"Hey," Cheney snapped, "what—"

"Shhh." Lenny's dad leaned over the desk with his head cocked slightly, listening to the noises from the phone, the clicks and pings and gurgles, scribbling down equations as he listened, sketching a waveform between them. When he was finished, he glanced back over what he'd written.

"I don't believe it," he said, in a small, weak voice. All of sudden he didn't look so tough anymore. In fact, he looked a little sick. All of the color drained out of his face, making it look kind of pasty and wrinkled on the surface, like a bowl of cream of mushroom soup that you'd pass over at the cafeteria line, and he put the pencil down, turned around very slowly, and stared at Lenny's mom.

"He's right," he said, in a funny little voice. "The frequencies match perfectly."

"I told you," Lenny said.

"But that's—that's impossible," Lenny's dad said. "How did you . . . how *could* you possibly—"

"I told you. I made it work."

"Son . . ." Lenny's dad shook his head. "You realize

that what you're describing violates every known law of physics. Why, the electrolytic transport alone would—"

"I thought of that," Lenny's voice said. "I read your notes. You gave up too easily. I formulated guanosine into a topical ointment—"

"Guanosine." Lenny's dad was already nodding. "Yes. Of course, for the superconductive properties. But—"

"Excuse me," Mr. Cheney said, still putting the pencils back in their holder. "What are you two talking about? What's this Von Friedrich experiment? Who's Purkinje?"

Lenny's dad ignored him. "Son, listen to me—"

"No," Lenny said, "*you* listen, Dad. I did this, okay? Me, by myself. While you and Mom were so busy working on your own projects and letting me get beat up at school because you told me to be myself, *I actually did this.*"

"Lenny, you don't understand. The hypothesis in my notes isn't stable—that's why I abandoned it. Even with the guanosine, you can't—"

"I love her, Dad. And I'm going to change her mind about me."

Dr. Cyrus shook his head in total confusion. "*What?*"

There was a click, and Lenny was gone.

# TWELVE ::: ZOOEY

"Ms. Andrews? Zooey? Are you feeling all right?"

I glanced up with a sense of certain doom. The voice belonged to Mrs. Emeritus, my third-period world history teacher. She was a massive, gray-haired monument of a woman, draped in a faded lavender dress, and she almost never rose out of her seat unless there was a fire alarm. But right now she seemed about ready to jump up and call an ambulance for me.

*If I really look that bad,* I decided, *it must be even worse than I thought.*

"I'm fine," I said, but the words came out sounding hoarse and unsteady. "I just need to sit down."

"I'll be the judge of that." Without taking her eyes off me, she hunched forward, gripping the edges of her desk and hoisting her great purple-clad bulk upward out of the chair. "You look absolutely green."

"Really, I'm okay."

"I won't stand for illness in in my classroom, Ms. Andrews. When you're my age, you can't afford to get sick." To demonstrate this, she reached down to the enormous bottle of hand sanitizer that she kept next to her economy-size box of Kleenex and squirted a glob into her palm, then added another squirt for good measure and began smearing it halfway up her quivering, ham-size forearms. "You march yourself down to the office and have Nurse Fitch take a look at you."

"Really," I said, "there's no reason—"

"Now, please, Ms. Andrews. Before you infect the lot of us."

"Yes, ma'am." There was no point arguing any further. Mrs. Emeritus was a germ fanatic. No matter what part of world history we were studying, she always found an opportunity to work in some mention of contagious disease. To hear her talk about it, Western civilization was one endless, sniveling bout of smallpox, tuberculosis, and polio, and it was nothing short of a miracle that we'd survived this long.

I left the classroom and walked down to the little office that Nurse Fitch kept around the corner from the teachers' lounge. When I got there, the door was half open, and I could already smell the bandages and rubbing alcohol.

"Who's there?" a voice asked.

"Zooey Andrews," I said, and stepped inside. It was a narrow rectangular space just big enough for a padded table and a counter with jars of cotton balls, Band-Aids, and gauze. A diagram of the human spine hung on the wall, illustrating the various ways that you could ruin your life by not standing up straight. Nurse Fitch herself stood in front of me, her hands on her hips.

"Well?" She was pale and skinny, with a beaklike nose and a lot of white-blond hair that she kept clamped in a bun so tight that it pulled her eyes back at the corners. "What is it?"

"Mrs. Emeritus sent me down," I said. "She told me I looked sick."

"I see." She put one hand on my forehead. "How do you feel?"

"Okay, I guess."

"Just okay?" She snapped on a rubber glove and pointed at the table behind me. "Take a seat."

"I'm really—"

"Say ahh." She peered into my mouth, listened to my lungs with a stethoscope, and wrapped a blood pressure cuff around my arm, pumping it up until my hand went numb. When she was finished, she released the pressure in a long, slow hiss, took off her stethoscope, and sat back on the stool.

"Well," she said, "it's probably just a virus. Who have you been kissing?"

"What?" I stared at her, feeling my cheeks burn. "Nobody!"

"Of course not." She picked up a pad of paper and started writing something. "Take this to the principal's office and call your parents to come pick you up."

"Wait," I said. "I can't go home."

She arched an eyebrow. "Excuse me?"

"My play starts this afternoon. I need to be there."

"Take the note." She held it out, waiting. "I've done my job. Now you do yours."

"Nurse Fitch," I said, struggling to keep my voice steady, "please." I looked at her closely, searching her narrow face for some trace of humanity. "I've been working on this play for the last two years. This afternoon's our first performance. I really need to be there. When it's over, I'll go straight home, I promise."

"Do you know what AMA stands for, Miss Andrews?"

I felt the shadow of hopeless dread come over me in a solid wave. "No, ma'am."

"Against medical advice." She pronounced it slowly, savoring every syllable. "When I worked at Chicago Memorial, we had a little girl just like you who came into the ER one night with symptoms like yours—nothing severe, mind you, just normal flu symptoms. The doctors wanted to keep her overnight for observation. But that little girl's parents felt it was more important that she make it to a ski trip that weekend, so they took her home—*against medical advice.*" She waited, pursing her lips. "And do you know what happened to her?"

"She was fine?" I asked hopefully.

"She died. One week later."

I stared at her. *"What?"*

"One week." Nurse Fitch nodded. "To the day."

"How?" My stomach was starting to churn again, and I felt the color draining out of my face. The lights seemed to be dimming, fading to black. "I mean, how did it happen?"

"The infection went systemic—took over her bodily functions and shut them down one at a time." Her eyes slipped downward as if she could see an x-ray of my own body coming undone from the inside. "First her kidneys, then her liver, then when it finally reached her heart—"

"Nurse Fitch . . ." I tried to step away, but she put one hand on my shoulder, gripping me tightly.

"What's the matter, dear?" she asked, leaning in close. "I thought you felt *fine.*"

"I think you'd better—"

"Better what?"

"I think you should—"

"Yes?"

"Watch out," I croaked. But it was too late. I felt everything in my stomach coming up all at once in a hot, stinging splash. Nurse Fitch let out a startled squawk and jerked away, tripping over the stool and hitting the floor with a thud, then scrambling back up again, the heels of her shoes skidding through the mess on the floor.

I clapped both hands over my mouth and stared at her, horrified. I wanted to say that I was sorry—I really did—but the words were locked in my throat. I just shook my head and blinked at her in shock. "I didn't—I mean—"

"Get out!" she shouted. *"Take your note and get out of here!"*

I picked up the note from the floor and backed out of the office.

# THIRTEEN : : : LENNY

"What was *that?*" I asked when the aftershocks had faded.

The astrovirus looked at me suspiciously. We'd left the bloodstream and were now floating somewhere in a lymph node in Zooey's left axillary area when the impact of whatever just happened had ripped through the tranquility like an earthquake.

"You're not really a virus, are you?" the astrovirus asked.

"*What?*" I frowned. "Yes, I am. I'm a—new mutation, like you said."

"Please." It made a disbelieving lip-fart and splashed me in the face mask with some lymph. "I might not be the smartest virus in the mix, but your chemical makeup is all screwy. Way more complex than any virus I ever met. Plus, I'm pretty sure you're wearing deodorant. And that phone call? Dude, come on. Dead giveaway."

"I don't know what you're talking about."

"Whatever," the virus said. "It's your call, but I don't hang with liars. 'Fess up now or I bail." It turned around and started swimming away.

"Okay, okay, wait." I shook my head. "You're right. I'm not a virus. I'm just a guy."

He turned around, sizing me up. "Little small for your age, aren't you?"

"I used nanotechnology to miniaturize my atomic structure."

"Whoa, nice one!" Now the astrovirus actually sounded impressed. "And I thought I was twisted. So what's the plan? You gonna infect her with something nasty?"

"What?"

"Colonize her bowel?"

"No!"

"So what's the plan?"

"I just need to tell her something."

The astrovirus just floated there in front of me for a second like it didn't understand. "Excuse me?"

"I need to talk to her."

"And you couldn't just, like, send her a text message?"

"It's not that simple."

"Oh, I'm sorry, you're right. It's so much easier to, like, shrink yourself down to microscopic level, impersonate a virus, and smuggle yourself up to her brain. What's your real name, anyway?"

"Lenny."

"Okay, Lenny, call me Astro, okay? That way we can at least get past this whole interspecies thing."

I stared at him for a second. "Maybe it's the lack of oxygen in the hemoglobin, but I think I'm seeing things." I squinted, pushed the diving mask up off my face for a second, and rubbed my eyes, but what I'd thought was a hallucination was becoming more and more real. When I'd first run into him down in the stomach, Astro had just been this gray, relatively amorphous, vaguely star-shaped blob. But now I realized he actually looked like a *guy*, with a chubby face, half-lidded eyes, an upturned nose, and a mouth that was twisted up into a kind of permanent half-smile. "You've really got a face?"

"Well, duh, dude. What did you think I was talking out of, my pores?"

"But, I mean"—I tried not to make it sound offensive—"you're a virus."

"So?"

"So I've looked at plenty of viruses under the microscope, and I've never seen one with a face before."

"Maybe you haven't looked close enough," Astro said. "You ever think of that, Linus Pauling?"

"No, but, I mean—" I shook my head. "Does everything down here have a face?"

"I dunno," he said, mimicking me perfectly. "Does everything *up there* have a face?"

"Yeah, but we're people."

"So, maybe viruses are just like little tiny people."

"Yeah, right."

"Why not? We reproduce like crazy and cause all kinds of trouble in the meantime. There are some uncanny similarities." He waited for me to argue, but when you put it like that, the comparison wasn't easy to dispute. "Anyway, tomato, to-mah-to. I gotta ask, that doorknob you were talking to—that was your dad, wasn't it?"

"Picked up on that, did you?"

"Viruses are pretty observant. What we lack in book learning, we make up for in street smarts. Another thing you seem to be sorely lacking, I might add."

"What's that supposed to mean?"

"I'm just saying—"

A sudden, low-throated snarling sound rose up from somewhere in the deep tissue, filling the lymph node with echoes and reverberations. I whirled around and stared up into the gray outer capsule above us, listening to all the weird autoregulatory noises of Zooey's body going about its business. I'd already gotten used to the continuous thump and whoosh of her heart and circulation, the sound of air billowing in and out of her lungs, the aftershocks of her voice like thunder far off in the distance, from way up in her larynx, although I could never make out the actual words.

But *this* noise was different—a menacing growl, like some primordial sea creature swimming up from the depths of the lymph to swallow us both.

"Gas bubble," Astro said. "You'll hear a lot more of those. She's getting hungry for lunch. What day is it?"

"Friday."

"Yikes. Chili day in the caf. How long are you planning on hanging out here?"

"As long as it takes," I said, flicking my eyes at the digital readout inside the mask. According to the display, I had a little more than three hours left before I started to get big again, but time passed differently on the inside. It seemed like I'd been here all day already, maybe longer.

"Well, if you're smart, you'll get out fast," Astro said. "Zooey loves chili, but it does stuff to her that I wouldn't wish on the worst vaccine in the system." He turned around and looked at me. "Which reminds me—on your way up to the cerebral cortex to whisper sweet nothings to your beloved, how exactly are you planning on sneaking through the blood-brain barrier?"

"The . . . ?" I opened my mouth to answer and snapped it shut again, stunned at my own stupidity. When it came to neural anatomy, the blood-brain barrier was Fort Knox—four hundred miles of narrow capillaries packed with epithelial cells whose sole purpose in life was to protect the brain from infection by keeping out large molecules like bacteria while letting other specific molecules through. If I'd been a molecule of alcohol, caffeine, or nicotine, I could've sailed right on in without a care in the world, but in my current situation, I'd have a better chance of sneaking a nuke through O'Hare Airport. "I didn't think of that."

"Yeah," Astro said, "that's what I figured. You can't just boogie into the hypothalamus and start telling neurons what to do. You wouldn't last five seconds up there."

"So what do we do?"

He grinned. "You're in luck. I know a guy. A steroid, his name's Lug. Not too bright, but he's lipid-soluble."

"Where do we find him?"

"That's the good news. He just happens to hang out with some pretty hot hormones nearby."

"Hormones?"

"*Oh* yeah."

I took in a breath. "Okay . . ."

"What?" He cocked an eyebrow at me. "You sure you're up to this?"

"Yeah," I said. "Why not? Let's go."

"Hold up a second," Astro said. "Are you telling me you want to get down with the *ovaries?* You want to kick it with some *estrogen?*"

I didn't want to, really, less and less with every second. But he was right—I wasn't going to get through the blood-brain barrier alone. Steroids like Lug, on the other hand, could slip right through the BBB, entering into the cerebrospinal fluid without ever having to tap the brakes. So in my bravest voice, I said, "Let's go."

"I'm warning you, Einstein. These ladies party pretty hard this time of the month. I mean, it can get *wild* down there. You might not make it back."

"You're a virus, right?"

"*I'm* a virus, yeah. But *you're* just some shrunk-down little punk who took a wrong turn at the esophagus. Fair warning: If things start going sideways, you're on your own."

"I'll take my chances."

"Fair enough," Astro shrugged. "Follow me."

# FOURTEEN ::: HARLAN

I was still in Mr. Cheney's office, trying to figure out how to make a graceful exit, when I looked out the window across the hall and saw Zooey backing out of the school nurse's office with a note her hand. Even from this distance, with her face turned away from me, I could see that she wasn't doing well. She looked shaky, a little unsteady on her feet, and she had to lean against the wall to keep her balance.

My first thought was, *Lenny, you tool. Are you doing this to her?*

"Mr. Williams?" Mr. Cheney cleared his throat, which

actually made the classic *harrumph* sound. I wondered if he practiced in front of a mirror. "Are we keeping you from something?"

"What? No, sir. No." I turned back to where Cheney was still sitting across from Lenny's parents. Lenny's dad was poised upright in his chair with that smacked-between-the-eyes look on his face. He kept staring at my cell phone, as if he somehow expected Lenny's voice to come back and keep explaining the process, and then up at Lenny's mother, who just kept blinking and shaking her head slowly back and forth.

I glanced back out the door. Zooey was gone, headed back to class. I hoped that she wasn't *really* sick, but if she was—

A hand fell on my arm, and I jumped, then turned and saw Lenny's dad standing over me. "Listen to me, Harlan. Do I have your complete attention?"

"Yessir."

"Good. Because I want you to tell me everything—do you understand? Every detail of every equation. I want to see his notes. How he did it, and how long the process is going to last, and most importantly, I want to know *where he is this very second*."

"Honey," Lenny's mom started. "Maybe—"

"Right now," Lenny's dad said, not taking his eyes off me. "Is that clear?"

I stared back at them. Part of me—the 1.0 version that still feared adults and what they could do to me—

wanted to spill my guts and tell them everything. I didn't even know where Lenny's notes were, but I could at least relay the tiny amount that he'd explained to me back in the lab.

But then, as I looked deeper into Lenny's father's eyes, I realized what was really bothering him. It wasn't that his son might be in danger.

It wasn't that Lenny might be endangering someone else.

It was that Lenny had done something that his father hadn't been able to do.

I didn't know Lenny's dad particularly well, but I knew him well enough to understand that when it came to something like this, being runner-up—especially to his own son—would drive him crazy. With the possible exception of his wife, Dr. Donald Cyrus was used to being the smartest one in the room, always.

That was when I knew what I had to do.

"Dr. Cyrus," I said, spreading my hands in front of me as if to show I had nothing to hide, "I'm sorry. This was all my idea, and it was a big mistake."

"What was?" he demanded. "What are you talking about?"

"Lenny didn't think you'd actually fall for it. But he promised he'd go along with the joke, so I—"

"Wait a minute." Lenny's dad glared at me. "Joke? You mean to tell me this whole thing was just a gag? He didn't really undergo the miniaturization process?"

"*Miniaturization* process?" Mr. Cheney said. "What in the world . . . ?"

"Of course not." I kept my attention on Lenny's dad, who was watching me very carefully now. He was still angry, but there was something else going on underneath the anger. It looked suspiciously like relief. "The process is . . ." I tried to think of the way Lenny would have said it. ". . . way too unstable. I mean, he found your notes, but he said that if a Nobel Prize winner like you couldn't make the process work, there was no way that he'd be able to do it."

"Well." Lenny's dad straightened his shoulders and nodded. "He's absolutely right about that. It goes without saying." He glanced back at Mr. Cheney. "There you have it. This whole thing was just a practical joke."

"So where is he then?" Lenny's mother asked.

"Who, Lenny? Oh, he's . . ." I paused. "He's in the auditorium. Helping Zooey and Aria get ready for the play. He's fine."

"Play? What play?"

"Come on, Susan. We've wasted enough time here." Lenny's dad was already taking her hand, looking at his watch, and gathering his coat from the rack by the door, then shooting a glance back at me. "I certainly hope you two are satisfied. You've disrupted our workday with your little prank, bringing us out here for nothing. I expected more of Lenny."

"I'm sorry," I said, getting up myself. For the first time in my life, I couldn't wait to get back to English class.

"Well, you certainly should be. Come on, Susan."

Hand in hand, they headed out of the office. But Lenny's mom was still looking at me sideways as she followed him out the door.

# FIFTEEN ::: ZOOEY

I was in the bathroom with my early dismissal note from the nurse's office, trying to gargle the nasty taste from my mouth, when another one of Martha Gelhorn-Smith's rules for success popped into my head.

*Rule #2: Sometimes you have to break the rules.*

I looked up at myself in the mirror, a little shocked. I wasn't normally a rule-breaker. In fact, I'd always been the kind of person who did what she was told. Even the play had been written in my spare time, *after* I'd finished my homework.

But something had changed, and I wasn't sure what. I felt different. Free, somehow. I thought about Nurse

Fitch sitting of the floor with her hair stuck to her fore-head, screaming at me, and I started to laugh.

"Rule number eleven," I told my reflection. "It doesn't matter whether if you're a rule-breaker or not—once you puke in somebody's face, there's nowhere to go but up."

When I got back to Mrs. Emeritus's classroom, she was talking about how the Black Death had laid waste to Europe, killing twenty-five million people in the Middle Ages. "Some of you might have heard of this horrific disease referred to by its other name," she said. "The bubonic plague."

Somebody giggled in the back of the classroom.

"The word *bubonic* comes from the word *bubo,* meaning 'swollen gland,' and—" Now there were several boys sniggering in the back, but Mrs. Emeritus was glaring at me. "Back so soon, Miss Andrews?"

"She said I was fine," I said.

"Really."

"Uh-huh."

I slipped back into my seat and listened to her talk about all the different unspeakable ways that the plague killed people. She was really getting into it, talking about rats and fleas and people dying in the streets. When the bell rang, I got up and grabbed my binder and textbook.

"Miss Andrews? Are you sure you're all right?"

"I'm fine," I shouted back, and without waiting for her response, I ducked back out the door.

That was when I saw the news crew, cameras and microphones and all, coming up the hall.

## SIXTEEN ∶∶∶ LENNY

Astro and I heard Zooey's ovaries a long time before we got to one. The pounding rhythm of what sounded like tribal electronica pulsated up through the fallopian tubes along with thousands of voices screaming, laughing, and cheering, getting steadily louder, like an all-girl rock concert going on somewhere inside the tubal vessels, until we came blasting through the ovarian artery and landed smack in the middle of the party.

For a second, I stood there looking around and trying to get my bearings. Like a lot of things I'd run into down here, the ovary—right or left, I wasn't sure which one we were in—was a lot bigger and noisier than I'd expected. The place was packed with moving bodies. Flashing disco lights and strobes pulsed off the walls, and the floor was made up of thousands of different-colored squares that lit up and pulsed in time with the music.

"Awesome, right?" Astro shouted. "I'm telling you, bro, nobody parties like these girls! *Nobody!*"

I'd had my doubts about coming down here, but he was right—I'd never been to a scene like this in my life. Granted, I'd never really been to any sort of party since Harlan had invited me to his seventh birthday at Chuck E. Cheese, but still . . .

"Go ahead!" Astro shouted. "What are you waiting for? Get out there and mingle. I'll go find Lug."

Before I could ask him where to start, something nudged into me from behind. When I turned around, a frantic sea of undulating bodies—curvaceous molecular clusters, colorful and bubbling, coiling and twisting around one another—started to push in around me, pressing up close on all sides. To my new, molecularly heightened senses, it all smelled like Juicy Fruit and papaya hair product.

"Woot!" one of them shouted, grabbing me and spinning me around. "Are you ready to get cah-*razy?*"

I looked straight at her, saw the molecule's face—big shimmering eyes with smiling lips and a bundle of blond hair swinging from side to side while she danced. She was wearing some kind of sleekly kinetic black membrane that clung to her curves, shimmering like an electric prom dress.

The music got louder and everybody started dancing. Off to the left, I saw Astro plunging right in the middle of it, jumping from one hormone molecule to another. The compound in front of me leaned in close, and I could feel the heat pouring off her in waves.

"I like your chemical makeup," I shouted.

"Thanks!" she shouted back. "What's your name?"

"Lenny." I evaluated her structure, trying not to be obvious about checking out the two hydroxyls swelling up out of her D ring. "You're . . . estriol, right?"

"Hey, that's right!" She looked impressed. "Have we met somewhere before?"

"I've read about you in books." That wasn't, strictly speaking, true—most of what I remembered came from a pretty embarrassing movie in sixth grade health class called *Some Body's About to Change!*.

The estriol squealed. "That's awesome! Have you met everyone?"

"Not yet."

We started making our way through the crowd, squeezing between compounds I only vaguely remembered from biology. Up ahead I saw clusters of more estriol, estradiol and estrone, progesterone, and aldosterone, all decked out to the nines, dancing and pressing up against me in a jouncing sea of high-energy hormones.

"Yo, Lenny!" Astro shouted, yanking me over. "Meet Lug!"

I looked up and saw a massive, ultrabuff molecule hunched over a table in the corner. At first glance, Lug looked to be half gym rat, half brick wall—slabs for shoulders, scrambled DNA for brains, tiny little eyes peering out suspiciously at his microscopic world. Underneath his spandex muscle shirt and black jeans, every part of him seemed to be testing the limits of the cellular membrane that encased his beefy heft.

When he saw me standing there, he leaned back, stretched, and flexed, and I realized that I was somehow

seeing him both as a chemical compound like the ones I'd studied under the microscope and a football player like the ones I helped with their homework.

"You the new virus?" he growled.

"Yeah."

"Heard you're looking for someone to get you across the BBB."

"That's right."

"What's in it for me?"

"I don't know," I said. "What do you want?"

"Glycogen. Twenty molecules up front, another fifteen when I get you to the other side."

"I don't usually carry that much on me," I said, glancing at Astro, who looked as helpless as I felt. "I mean, I could get some, but . . ."

Lug was already losing interest. "Then we got nothing to talk about."

"Wait," I said. I had an idea, but I was going to have to work fast. "Just give me a second. I really need—"

"Get lost, virus, before I break you in half." He started to turn away.

That was when I grabbed him.

# SEVENTEEN ::: HARLAN

I was on my way out of Mr. Cheney's office when the bell rang for the end of third period, and a moment later I heard a commotion behind me in the hall.

Looking back, I saw Zooey talking to a TV news crew, which had already started unloading their gear in the entryway, unspooling long black pythons of electrical cable. I remembered what she'd told me earlier about reporters from WCRW coming to do a piece on the play.

"Harlan?"

I looked back. It was Lenny's mom. She'd broken away from Lenny's dad, who was already standing half-way down the hall, waiting for her.

"Who was Lenny talking about?" his mother asked.

"What?"

"That ... girl that Lenny mentioned. The one he's supposedly so ... fixated on." She glanced at one of the posters for *Escape Claus,* hanging on the wall behind her, and then looked over at Zooey with the camera crew, but Zooey's head was turned the other way, and Lenny's mom didn't see her face. "Is that the one who's putting on this Christmas play?"

For a second I just stared at her, not quite able to believe my ears. For the last five years, Zooey Andrews had literally been the only girl that Lenny had ever talked about. In fact, he'd talked about her so much that even I had actually gotten sick of hearing about her ... and I *liked* her. I knew that he'd told his mom and dad about her too, over and over, year after year—mentioned her specifically by name a million times at the dinner table. One year on Valentine's Day he'd actually created this weird pink chemical gas, lighter than air, that spelled out her name in twenty-foot-high floating letters over the front yard. It had lingered there for almost three days and left a big stain on the grass. His dad had to hire a lawn service to scrub it off. I don't think Zooey ever saw it.

"Why do you want to know?" I asked.

"Because I'm his mother. And if this ... person is distracting him from his studies, then I think we need to have a talk with her."

"Why don't you try having a talk with *him* for once?" I asked.

"Are you insinuating that we don't communicate?"

"No, I'm saying you don't talk."

"Susan!" Lenny's dad called from the door, pacing with impatience. "Can we go, please? *Tempus fugit!*"

"I'm coming." She turned back to me. "For your information, Harlan, Leonard and I have very rewarding conversations every day."

"About what? Strange quarks? Subatomic particles? Honestly, Dr. Cyrus, when was the last time you asked him about his feelings?"

She narrowed her eyes. "Feelings?"

"Yeah," I said, "you know—those things that aren't thoughts?"

"Please," she said, "spare me your semantics. Lenny knows that he can come to us whenever he likes. I think we've made that abundantly clear to him in the past." She stared at me. "And right now, between this untenable bullying situation and whatever else is going on, I think he's got more to worry about than feelings."

I just shook my head. "Right."

"Harlan, I have to say, I'm quite disappointed in you as well. If you were a true friend, you'd be more worried about him."

"Oh, that's funny, coming from you."

"I beg your pardon?"

"You guys just go on living your lives, doing whatever you want and plowing right ahead with your experiments or whatever, but do you ever think about what any of it does to him? Do you ever think about the consequences?"

"I've heard just about enough of this." Lenny's mom crossed her arms. "Where did you say he was right now? The auditorium?"

"Yeah, but—"

"Let's go see him right now." She threw another glance down the hall at Lenny's dad. "Don? There's been a change of plans."

That was when I realized I'd made a big mistake.

# EIGHTEEN : : : ZOOEY

The TV crew wanted to set up in the auditorium, to get what they called "bump shots" of the stage and costumes for the evening broadcast. I told them that the play wasn't supposed to start until three thirty, but the reporter, a guy named Ted, told me that he could get what they needed now.

"That might be a problem," I said. "See, the auditorium's also the gym, and—"

"We'll work around it." Ted popped a breath mint, flashed a smile so white that it hurt my eyes a little, and gestured me forward. "You're Joey Daniels, you said? The little girl in charge of all this?"

I gritted my teeth. "Zooey Andrews."

"Right." He waved to the cameraman and the sound

guy and they came trailing up the hall, dragging wires along after them. "Listen, sweetie: I know it's exciting having us here. Just try to relax. When we get there, I'll ask you a few questions. Just try to speak clearly and don't look directly at the camera, okay?"

I shot a glance at the crowded hallway. Classes were changing, and the bad news was that Harlan and I were supposed to be starting gym in about two minutes. I didn't think that Mr. Shoenwald was going to be too happy to see a news crew showing up during class. Even worse, I was pretty sure that, unlike my other teachers, old Shovelhead wasn't going to excuse me from class to deal with the reporter and cameras. Getting an excuse from gym was ridiculously hard, and usually required a doctor's note, if not a broken limb or a blood-spurting injury—either of which would've been preferable to having a TV crew videotaping me running around in a pair of gym shorts.

"Where are we going?" Ted the reporter asked. "Which way?"

"I'd be happy to escort you," a voice behind me said, and I turned around to see Aria standing behind me. She was dressed in her Mrs. Claus costume, boots and full stage makeup, which was a surprise since the play wasn't supposed to start until after school.

"Aria?" I said, staring at her. "What are you doing?"

"Aria Keen—so pleased to meet you." She practically knocked me down reaching out to shake Ted's hand.

"Actress, singer, ingenue." She handed him a glossy black-and-white headshot. "All of my contact information's on the back."

Ted glanced at the photo, then up at her. "You're the one who called my office?"

"Yes," Aria said modestly, "that's right. Now if you want to follow me . . ."

"Wait a second," I said. "*You* called them?"

"Well, of course," Aria said. "Do you think that TV people just happen to come to middle school plays? You have to pursue them." She smiled back at Ted and his cameraman and sound technician. "If we start walking now, we can get there before class starts."

"Aria," I said, "wait."

She turned back to me with a pasted-on smile. "Do you really think you should be here today, Zooey? You don't look well at all."

"I'm fine," I said, but they were already moving again, and I had no choice but to chase after them, trying to catch up, even though my stomach was making weird burbling noises and I wasn't sure I should be running.

We were almost to the gym when I saw Harlan pushing his way toward me, but he wasn't alone. There were two adults following him, and they both looked weirdly familiar, like two halves of somebody I knew from school. Harlan didn't look too happy to be with them.

In fact, I could've sworn he was mouthing the word "run."

## NINETEEN : : : LENNY

"Dude," Astro said in a low voice as he backed away, "are you out of your mind?"

It was too late to turn back now. I'd already jammed Lug up against the wall of the ovary, shoving both hands through his membrane, straight into the deepest recesses of his molecular structure, where the atoms came together. He was so big that I had to stand on my tiptoes to reach in, but I found what I was looking for fast enough, and when I got there, I didn't hesitate. Grabbing a hydroxyl in one hand and a methyl group in the other, I gripped them as hard as I could and pulled. They came off their respective nitrogen bindings with a loud pop and a hiss, like somebody cracking open a fresh soda. Lug jumped up, looking startled, and got right up in my face.

"Kid, you just signed your death warrant."

"Hold still," I said. "You don't want me to mess this up."

"What are you—"

"Be quiet and let me work." Flashing back on what I remembered about my dad's molecular engineering textbooks, I started switching up his valences and replacing atoms onto the newly available bindings. When I finished, Lug stood there motionless for a long moment.

"Whoa . . ." he said. "What did you do?"

"Changed a few things around," I said. "You're not a steroid anymore."

"I feel different." He looked down at his rearranged chemical structure. "I feel . . . better."

"Good."

"*Smarter.*"

"Uh-huh."

"More energy, and—"

"Yeah," I said, "that makes sense."

"—I want to dance."

"What?"

"*Dance!*"

He spun and roared into the crowd, and they roared back at him in delight as he pivoted around to look at me, a huge grin on his face. His eyes blazed with new light, new awareness, and probably new ideas for ways of putting my life in jeopardy. Astro leaned over and whispered in my ear.

"What did you do?"

"Just some basic atomic restructuring," I said. "I turned him into a caffeine molecule."

"Oh." Astro looked out at the crowd, where Lug was jumping up and down and waving furiously at me. "And that's a good thing?"

"I think he's going to help us now."

"I think he wants to dance."

"He's already dancing," I said.

"No, I mean, I think he wants *you* to dance."

"I can't—"

"Dude, *do* it. You do not want this guy as an enemy. Especially now that you've turned him into a living can of Red Bull. Now he's huge, supersmart, *and* completely amped out of his mind?" He shook his head. "I'd start dancing."

I pushed my way out into the crowd. After a few steps I realized that something was wrong with my oxygenation system, or maybe there wasn't enough hemoglobin down here, because as the room got crowded, it was becoming harder to breathe. When I got out to the middle of the dance floor, the last thing I remember was Lug grabbing me and wrapping me in a big sweaty hug. As he whipped me around, squeezing me harder, I realized I was in trouble.

My lungs cramped and a blade of pain hit me across the sternum.

Then everything went black.

# TWENTY ::: HARLAN

I was trapped outside the gymnasium with Lenny's parents, sandwiched between a flood of kids coming out and the TV news crew trying to fight their way in, when I felt someone grab my arm. It was Blake Hartman, captain of the football team.

"Hey, man," Blake shouted. "Have you seen Lenny around?"

I saw Lenny's mom turn at the sound of his name. She looked Blake up and down, saw his muscles and football jersey, and jumped nimbly to her own conclusions. "Who are you?" she demanded. "Are you one who's been picking on him?"

"What? No." Blake flipped open his notebook and pulled out an unfinished algebra worksheet. "Lenny always helps me with my math."

"Helps you with it," Lenny's dad said, "or does it for you?"

I closed my eyes and thought, *Oh, Lenny. I can't believe you have to live with this.*

Blake, meanwhile, looked genuinely bewildered. "It's not like that. He actually explains it to me so I get it, you know? Like when two trains pass each other at sixty miles a hour and stuff like that?" He shot another glance at Lenny's parents and started backing away. "Anyway, I gotta go."

Lenny's mother watched him leave, then turned to face Lenny's dad. "I told you we should have considered private school."

"Next year," Lenny's dad muttered. "Brixton Academy."

"How about right after holiday break?"

"Even better."

The doorway had cleared, and the three of us made our way into the gym.

I should've known we were in trouble from the second I got inside.

The badminton nets were put away, the gymnastic mats had been rolled up, and the retractable wooden risers were pushed back into the wall, leaving the whole gym floor completely empty. On the opposite side, I saw

Aria Keen—who for some reason was already dressed in her Mrs. Claus costume—leading the camera crew toward the stage, where the curtains were drawn over the *Escape Claus* set. Zooey was following along behind them, looking sick. She was going to feel a whole lot sicker if Lenny's parents found out who she was.

"I don't see Lenny," his mom said, and glared at me. "Where is he, Harlan?"

I was about to admit the whole thing was a lie when the curtains parted and Mr. Shoenwald stepped out in his too-tight nylon running shorts and rippling biceps, hands on hips, staring down on us like a bronzed king surveying his domain.

"Who or what," Lenny's dad asked, "is *that* Neanderthal?"

I felt a cold, dull sense of misery drape itself over my shoulders like a wet towel. "That's our gym teacher."

Shovelhead bent over and started doing something with an iPod and some wires, plugging in cords to a set of speakers at the corner of the stage. Behind us, the rest of the kids in fourth-period gym were straggling their way in, dragging their feet and complaining every step, trying to take up as much time as possible before the last bell rang.

"Let's go, people," Shovelhead bawled down at us and clapped his hands together. The noise rang out like a gunshot. "Get changed and get your butts out here. I've got a special surprise for you today." He turned and

132

stared at the reporter and the cameraman making their way up on stage. "What's going on here, some kind of press conference?"

I rolled my eyes and looked back at Lenny's parents. "I'll be right back."

"They're from WCRW," Zooey was telling Mr. Shoenwald when I got close enough to hear. "They're taping a segment on the show this afternoon."

"I don't care if they're covering the Winter Olympics," Shovelhead snapped. "I need you suited up and ready in two minutes, Andrews—you got me? Or the next performance you'll be giving is two forty-five detention."

That was when Zooey turned around and saw me. Her eyes were dilated, and her face was flushed bright red, like she was getting a fever. "Harlan?"

"Hey," I said, and pointed at Aria, who was talking with both hands to the TV reporter. "What's Aria doing?"

"Apparently . . ." Zooey let out a breath. "I don't know. I guess she set this whole thing up herself without telling anybody."

"Are you okay?"

"Yeah, I'm . . . fine."

"You don't look so good."

"I'm just a little hot, that's all." She fanned herself. "Is it hot in here or is it just me?"

"Um," I said. "Listen, Zooey—"

"Sixty seconds!" Shovelhead bellowed, clutching the stopwatch that dangled around his neck next to his whistle, and Aria and the news crew disappeared behind the curtain.

"I should go with them," Zooey said, but Shovelhead just glared at her, arms crossed over his barrel chest. I'm not sure what happened next, except that Zooey just seemed to teeter backwards, as if she'd suddenly lost her balance and started to fall. I just barely managed to catch her arm before she would've tripped over one of the footlights. Touching her was a shock. Her skin wasn't just warm—it was *blazing*.

"You sure that you don't need to go see the school nurse or something?" I asked.

"I was just there. I'm fine."

"Okay, sorry. Jeez."

"No, it's just—" She shook her head. "I can't afford to be sick today, that's all. Today is huge."

"I know." I was starting to feel more nervous myself. "It'll be fine."

Shovelhead blasted his whistle again, louder than ever, and we both looked up, wincing.

"Let's go, people! *Now!*"

"Okay," I said, "I'll meet you back here."

Zooey nodded and I ducked into the locker room. Once I'd changed into my shorts and T-shirt, I pulled my cell phone out of my gym bag and stepped around the corner into the empty showers to dial Lenny's number. It rang three times, and his voice answered.

"Hello, this is Lenny—"

"Lenny," I said, "listen, it's me—"

"—I'm sorry, but I can't take your call right now. Leave me a message at the tone and I'll get back to you as soon as possible."

"Hey," I said, "I don't know what you're doing in there, but Zooey doesn't look so great. Call me back as soon as you get this." I tried to think of anything else to say. "And whatever you're doing in there, maybe you should just, I don't know, dial it down a little?"

Then I hung up.

When I came back out of the gym, the news crew had pulled the curtains aside to reveal the North Pole set in all its glory. Aria was standing center stage, demonstrating her choreography for Ted the reporter, her gown shimmering as it swirled around her legs.

Down on the gym floor, it was business as usual. I saw all the girls lined up on one side in their shorts and T-shirts, looking back at the guys. Zooey was at the end of the line, but she didn't look like herself at all. Her cheeks and neck were still all flushed, and she was just staring at me. When I mouthed the words "You okay?" she didn't say anything back.

"Okay, donkeys and donkettes," Shovelhead said. He was always calling us stuff like that, or else just *you guys* and *you females*. "Today we're going to be starting a new unit, which I know you're all going to be very excited about—square dancing."

Everybody groaned. There'd been rumors that the school was going to introduce square dancing as part of some new state requirement—maybe we weren't getting our recommended daily allowance of humiliation—but nobody could quite believe they'd actually go through with it. Regardless of where you stood on the topic of physical education, making a bunch of eighth-graders spin each other around to "Turkey in the Straw" definitely qualified as cruel and unusual punishment.

"Yeah, I know—awesome, right?" Shovelhead said with a little smile, and made a fist in front of his face, squeezing until the veins popped out. "*Awesome.*" I realized that he was actually enjoying this in a big way. "Now, we're gonna start by going through some basic steps with the music, and then everybody can come out here and try it together. Can I get a volunteer from both sides? How about you females?"

The girls all took a step back and looked down at their sneakers.

All except Zooey.

She stood motionless, her chin tilted up so that her hair fell back across her shoulders.

"Okay, great," Shovelhead said, and clapped his hands. "Hey, Andrews, that's great. How about you fellas? Don't all volunteer at once." His cocky little smile had become a big chip-toothed grin. He'd started rubbing his hands together like he did right before officiating a particularly vicious wrestling match. "Come on, guys—she's not gonna bite. Are you, Miss Andrews?"

Zooey didn't answer. She just stood there, staring at me, her face flushed bright red. Something was definitely going on inside her. Her mouth was just slightly open, and I realized that she was breathing in this funny way, so I could actually see her shoulders and chest going up and down. She actually looked like she *might* bite.

*Lenny, you idiot,* I thought. *What are you doing in there?*

"Okay, Miss Andrews, since these guys can't seem to grow some guts, why don't you just go ahead and pick somebody?"

I shut my eyes. I knew what was going to happen before she even took the first step.

Zooey walked over and grabbed my hand.

# TWENTY-ONE ::: ZOOEY

The truth is, I don't recall very much about what happened after that.

I remember I was burning up, and these weird hot and cold chills kept prickling up between my shoulder blades and the back of my neck. My heart was pounding so hard that I could feel it in my throat. I didn't feel sick exactly, just dizzy and distant, like I was watching the whole thing through a fishbowl.

I kept telling myself that if I could just get through this without passing out, I might even get a chance to talk to Ted the reporter before they left the set.

That was when I saw Harlan standing there, staring at me.

What I felt next, I can't describe. It was like something else inside of me just took over, like millions of packets of Really Bad Judgment pills were bursting open. My mind—what was left of it—flashed to sixth grade health class, where phrases like "raging hormones" were tossed around like a joke. It wasn't so funny now that my legs seemed to be moving on their own, carrying me across the gym floor toward Harlan.

Like I said, I don't remember much after that.

But it doesn't matter.

It all showed up on TV anyway.

# TWENTY-TWO ::: LENNY

Looking back, I'm not exactly sure when everything spun out of control, but I'm pretty sure it started when Lug stage-dived into a sea of raging estrogen.

I'd somehow managed to squirm away from him and regain consciousness after being squeezed half to death and tossed into the air. As my head cleared, I saw swarms of ecstatic hormones sweeping forward to embrace Lug, catching him and passing him around, screaming while the music got louder and faster, building to a frantic crescendo. Lug disappeared and a second later he popped back up on the far side of the ovary, waving for me to join him.

"Go on!" Astro shouted, punching me in the shoulder. "They want you to stage dive!"

"I can't! There's no air!"

"What?"

"There's not enough hemoglobin!" I pointed at him. "What about you?"

"No way, man! It's all you out there!"

Now the entire room was cheering for me to jump. I managed to get up onto the table, felt the mob swelling closer, and sucked in a deep breath. My heart was pounding fast. In spite of my recent brush with light-headedness or maybe because of it, I actually felt pretty good. The whole ovary was rocking hard enough that I could feel it trembling around me. If this had been a real party, the cops would have shown up already to shut things down, but down here on the molecular level, things were just getting started.

*I'm pretty sure this is what they mean by "chemical imbalance,"* I thought, and took the plunge. Estrogen and progesterone lunged forward to catch me, and the whole ovary went insane all over again, howling and roaring while the hydroxyls and methyl groups held me up and passed me around above their heads.

Astro got up on the table and started chanting. "Len-ny! Len-ny!"

I struggled to the surface, but the crowd just sucked me back in. Lights were flashing faster above my head, whole galaxies and nebulae exploding to life. My head spun and I grabbed a quick breath as the party went into overdrive. Everything around me was whipping itself into a state of near hysteria, but somehow, against all odds, I was grinning. I wasn't Lenny Cyrus anymore— I was somebody completely new and different, and maybe dangerous. I was Lenny Cyrus, Supervirus. As the music got louder I felt myself giving in to the euphoria, deep down on the chemical level, letting the energy of the moment carry me forward in a way I'd never done in the outside world.

On the far side of the crowd, Lug was moving faster, his massive, supercharged bulk building speed and power, feeding into the chaos. He was springing up into the air, pumping his fists, waving me forward. Electricity crackled through the open space and hit me like a jolt of pure caffeine, which I guess it might have been. Whatever he'd brought to the party, it was infectious.

The space around us was hot and getting hotter.

Things were definitely getting out of hand, and I knew it, but I couldn't stop, even if I'd wanted to.

That was when the roof caved in.

# TWENTY-THREE ::: HARLAN

Zooey's hand felt like it was about a hundred and fifty degrees as she pulled me out onto the gym floor, leading me forward until we stood in the middle between the two lines of guys and girls. Up on stage, Shovelhead was describing the various square dancing moves from the seventeenth century or whenever it was invented, but I couldn't think about that now. Zooey's face was about six inches away, her cheeks blazing red, with those blue eyes locked in on mine. On both sides I could hear the other kids giggling and whispering to each other, egging her on, but she didn't seem to notice.

She tilted her head down a little so she was looking at me from the tops of her eyes, and bit her lip. "I'll lead."

"Uh, okay, but—"

"Here we go," Shovelhead bellowed from up on stage. "I'm gonna start the music, and all you two have to do is listen to the caller and do the moves as he says them. If you get stuck, I'll help you." He reached up to the iPod that he'd hooked to the speakers. "Ready?"

He pushed the button and the music started playing—fiddle and guitar and some guy from Kentucky telling me to swing my partner round and round—but Zooey ignored it completely. For a second she just stood there, as still as a statue, burning up and practically panting.

"Come on, you two," Shovelhead said, "don't be shy! Step up, Harlan. Like I said, she's not going to—"

Zooey grabbed me with both arms and pulled me close up against her, swinging me around so fast that my sneakers actually left the floor. Her body was coiled tight, and I could feel her heart pounding against mine, hard and fast. Her skin was kicking off heat like an intense August day, the kind that overwhelms you and sucks your breath away from the moment you step outside.

"Okay," I said, "this is kind of ... close, don't you think?"

"Come on," she whispered into my ear. Her voice sounded husky and totally different, not a girl's voice at all but maybe that of a grown woman, or possibly some kind of vampire. "Let's dance."

"Zooey, I can't br—"

"Shut up."

"Okay. Shutting up." I tried to keep up, but all of a sudden this wasn't square dancing—it was more like some kind of no-holds-barred mixed martial arts. I tried to pull back, but she wouldn't let go. She gripped me tighter, one hand on my butt, one running up through my hair, so I could feel her fingernails scratching against my scalp.

The kids had all completely stopped talking. When Zooey spun me around again, I saw they were all staring

at us. Even Shovelhead had broken off his steady stream of hilarity and just stood there with his mouth sagging open like a cave leading nowhere, while Zooey whirled me in another foot-scrabbling, butt-grabbing circle.

We spun around again, and that was when I saw it.

Up on stage, the camera crew had stopped filming the sets for *Escape Claus* and started taping us. I had no idea how long they'd been at it, but I was pretty sure they'd caught the whole thing on film.

My heel caught on a stack of wrestling mats in the corner, and Zooey and I both went tumbling backwards, me on my back, Zooey on top of me, knocking all the air out of my lungs. I stared straight up, fighting to catch my breath. But Zooey wasn't getting up. Her glasses had slipped off, and her eyes bored straight down into mine, overloaded and blazing with that crazy blue fire.

"Zooey, what—"

She leaned down, narrowing the distance between us until I could feel her breath against my face, coming closer, her lips approaching mine.

"*Lenny*," she said.

"Wait," I said. "*What?*"

The music cut off.

The silence was deafening. It was like somebody had set off a bomb and left us lying there in the shock waves. Zooey sat up fast, some of the redness fading from her cheeks. She picked up her glasses and settled them back on her nose, then looked up at the stage, where Shovelhead was standing next to the iPod with his mouth still hanging wide open. For the first time in history, he didn't have a word to say.

"Harlan?" Zooey's eyes cleared, and she stood up, catching her breath. "What . . . *was* that?"

"I have no idea."

She swallowed and took a step back. The other kids were still staring at us as she turned and ran toward the girls' locker room.

"Zooey, wait—"

But she was already gone.

# TWENTY-FOUR ⋮ ZOOEY

When I got to the locker room, I ran straight the showers, turned the water on freezing cold, and stood there, fully clothed, letting the icy needles spray down over my upraised face and trickle down my back. Normally I like my showers hot, but at the moment this was exactly what I needed.

My head finally started to clear. What exactly had just happened back there? Compared to this, getting sick felt normal. At least with the flu, you knew what to expect. I felt like somebody had kidnapped me and was dragging me through the most embarrassing circumstances imaginable:

A) I had grabbed Harlan's butt during square dancing and tried to kiss him in front of TV news crew, who had probably filmed the whole thing.

B) That was pretty much it.

"Zooey?" asked a voice outside the shower.

I took off my glasses, wiped my eyes, and looked out. Aria was standing there in her Mrs. Claus gown, peering in at me with an expression of . . . concern.

"Sweetie, are you okay?"

I stepped out of the shower with my hair in my face, dripping on the floor, hugging myself and shivering. "Do I look okay?"

"Well, no. Not exactly. But we can fix you up. I've got some dry clothes in my locker, a hair dryer, and some revitalizing moisture mist. We could—"

"Aria, what are you doing?"

She stopped. "What do you mean?"

"You invited the news team here without telling me, you put on your costume and hijacked my interview . . ." My teeth were chattering, and I tried to get control of it, but that only made it worse. "Now you're here pretending to be nice to me. I mean, what gives?"

She laughed without quite smiling, a cold chuckling noise that echoed off the wet tiles around us. "Zooey, no offense, but did you see yourself out there? What you were doing with Harlan Williams? I'd say you're the one who should be explaining."

I tried to answer but couldn't think of anything to say. She didn't seem to mind.

"Poor Zooey," she said, and leaned forward to pat me on the shoulder. "It's all right. I'm going to take care of everything. You'll see."

"Wait a second." I pulled away from her. Scheming and being a prima donna I could handle, but this new shoulder-patting development was downright disturbing. "Aria, I don't *want* you to take care of everything."

"Zooey, I don't think you know what you looked like out there. It wasn't pretty."

"I'm the writer and director. Looking pretty isn't a prerequisite."

"But being sane is," she said. "And slow dancing with Harlan Williams in front of the entire gym class doesn't exactly qualify as sanity, does it? Or have they changed the definition since I checked *Webster's Unabridged?*" Without waiting for an answer, she reached into the pocket of her gown for a page of notes. "Now, I've got a few choreography ideas that I'd like to try out before this afternoon."

I finished wiping off my glasses, put them back on, and stared at her. "Aria, what's this really about?"

"I'm sorry?"

"You seem pretty well prepared to step into the limelight."

"*Rule number five,*" she quoted. "*Always be ready to assume a position of leadership.*"

"Wait." I gave her a look. "You read Martha Gelhorn-Smith's memoir?"

"I listened to the audiobook."

"Right," I said, and managed a smile. Hearing her talk like this was actually weirdly reassuring, like whatever passed for normalcy had returned to our relationship. As long as she didn't try to pat my shoulder again, I figured I'd be fine.

"Don't you want to hear my ideas for Harlan's entrance?" Aria asked innocently.

"Maybe later." The truth was that I still wanted to figure it out myself. "Just make sure you're ready for the show at three thirty. It's noon already."

"Oh, I'll be ready," she said. "Just be sure *you* are."

"I'm fine," I said, just my stomach gave a long, loud growl.

It was almost lunch, and I suddenly realized that despite everything that had just happened, I was hungrier than I'd been in my entire life.

# TWENTY-FIVE ⋮⋮⋮ LENNY

At first I thought the whole ovary was collapsing on top of us. Rippling waves of leukocytes came tumbling down from overhead like an avalanche, blocking out everything and stopping the party cold.

All at once the lights came up.

"Everything all right over here?"

"It's Whitey," the estriol molecule in front of me murmured, and all the other estrogen compounds started trying to look innocent and make excuses as hundreds of white blood cells—leukocytes in stark white membranes—came pouring in through the vessels, surrounding the hormones and herding them into the middle of the ovary.

"You," the white blood cell in front of me barked, pointing straight at me with what looked like a combination of a billy club and a cattle prod. "Authorization, now."

"I don't—"

"He's with me," Lug said.

The leukocyte in charge didn't look impressed. "Zip it, alkaloid. This isn't your fight."

"I'm just saying—"

"Virus!" another of them yelled, and the estrogens all backed away, creating an open space around Astro. I saw three leukocytes grabbing him and slamming him against the ovary wall. He didn't look particularly intimidated.

"Don't waste your time," he muttered as the white blood cells clapped cuffs to every pair of his tendrils. "You guys can't touch me and you know it."

"Re-education center, now." The leukocyte in front of me grabbed my arms, taking a long look at my swim fins, the shredded diving suit, and mask. "You too, bug. You're in the wrong place at the wrong time. Cuff 'em and ship 'em both to One Kay."

I started to argue, but then a pair of slippery-feeling

handcuffs encircled my wrists. They felt rubbery, but when I tried to pull out of them, the spiral polymer only tightened around me in a double helix—DNA strands. They were actually using Zooey's genetic material to lock me up.

I looked around and saw a low-slung white transport sitting at the entrance to the ovarian vein. It looked like a big semitransparent bubble. Two of the white blood cells swung me around and shoved me into the back. I was still trying to protest when they jammed Astro in next to me and slammed the hatch.

"Don't worry about it," Astro muttered. "Reeducation center's a joke. My lawyer will have us out of here faster than you can say 'metabolic uptake.'"

I wasn't so sure, and I was about to say so when the headset on my ear started to vibrate. With my hands bound, I managed to nudge my cheek against the On switch, activating the phone.

"Hello?"

"Lenny?" Harlan's voice sounded panicked. "Things are really bad here, man!"

"Yeah?" I said, my head thumping off the seat cushion behind me as the transport shot up through the ovarian vein, hurtling forward along the curve of the vessel wall. "It's not exactly Disneyland down here, either."

"Zooey's gone completely haywire."

"Okay, I meant to warn you about that," I told him.

"You're probably going to notice some difference in her behavior. Her metabolic uptake is speeding up, so you may notice her appetite increasing. Maybe she'll eat more chicken nuggets at lunch."

"Dude, we just had square dancing in gym class and she tried to kiss me. Her face is all flushed and she's breathing weird. It's like she's possessed. *What are you doing to her?*"

"Wait," I said, "go back—you almost *kissed* her?"

"*She* almost kissed *me!*"

"What's the difference?"

"There's a big difference!" Harlan shouted, and his voice started to crack a little around the edges, as if he were going through a second puberty right here on the phone with me. "You think I would do that to you? I know how you feel about her, man. I'd never pull something like that!" He inhaled a breath and I could hear him trying to calm himself down. "Look—I don't know why she's behaving like this, seriously. It's like she's turned into Were-Zooey or something."

"Okay, just calm down," I said. "I think I know what happened. I was down in the ovaries—"

"Dude, what are you doing in her *ovaries?*"

"Just . . . let me finish, okay? We're trying to find a steroid to get us across the blood-brain barrier, and it's really difficult, so we went down to the ovaries to—"

"Who's *we?* Who's with you in there?"

"Just this virus I met," I said. "It's not important."

"Hey!" Astro said from beside me, looking hurt.

"Things got a little out of control because I converted this steroid into a caffeine molecule and he started mixing it up with the estrogen and progesterone, and the white blood cells had to come and break it up, but everything should be calming down soon."

"Oh, they're calming down, all right," Harlan said. "Zooey's in the girls' locker room right now and she won't come out."

I tried to think, but it was hard to clear my head when the leukocytes' transport was careening back up the vein at what felt like Mach 3. Up ahead I saw a massive gray tower approaching in the distance, tall and flat and curved outward like some kind of modern skyscraper. The sign in front of it read I KIDNEY. Swerving toward it, we bounced up toward a checkpoint, skidding to halt in front of the booth with another leukocyte standing inside.

"Two more for cellular reeducation," the white blood cell in front muttered.

"These the two from the ovary?" the leukocyte in the booth asked.

"Uh-huh."

"Heck of a mess down there from what I heard. Hormonal rioting, unauthorized steroid release, free radicals on the loose . . ." The white blood cell in the booth sounded disgusted. "They'll be sorting this out all afternoon."

The transport swung inside, dipping through a series of narrow vessels until we stopped at the end of a long gray tunnel.

"Out," the driver ordered, hauling Astro and me from the transport.

"Look, Harlan," I said. "I have to go. I'll call you later, okay?"

"Just do me a favor and don't mess anything else up while you're in there."

"Thanks for your concern," I said.

*Click*—he was gone.

We hustled down the hall to a giant freight elevator that hauled us straight up into the honeycombed levels of 1 Kidney. Rising up, I looked through the transparent wall and saw millions of little cubicles with individual renal cells slaving away. None of them even seemed to notice as we passed.

"We're going to be fine," Astro said. "Just be chill and I'll get us out of this."

The doors swung open on a huge horseshoe-shaped room full of squabbling voices. Everywhere I looked, thousands of viruses, bacteria, amino acids, and fat cells were packed in tightly, squabbling and trying to make themselves heard. Most were restrained like Astro and me, either cuffed or bracketed directly to the walls and benches where they sat, but a few of them had gotten loose and were running around pleading their case to anybody who would listen.

"Same thing every time," Astro groaned and rolled his eyes. "Never changes."

"Okay, listen up!" a leukocyte in front shouted, and the noise inside the room faded a little. "Welcome to biochemical reeducation. I need all infectious and possibly infectious organisms over on this side. Everybody else, stay where you are. We've got a brief orientation video and then we'll start with individual reassignment."

I leaned over to Astro. "What do I do?"

"Stick with me." He stood up and I followed him down the row, toward a long line of molecules gathering in the far corner. A small army of leukocytes were standing at attention, shuttling us forward.

"Keep moving," the one in charge snapped. "Viruses on the left, bacteria on the right, two orderly lines, you know the drill . . ."

"Watch it, bro," Astro muttered as we stepped into formation on the left side, shuffling along behind a rotavirus and what might have been the last of the chickenpox that Zooey'd had when she was twelve. The line rounded a corner, muttering and complaining, and filed through another, narrower entranceway. "They talk a good game, but since we're viruses, Whitey knows they can't—"

*Thump!*

"Hey." Astro turned and snapped a glance back at the wall that had slammed shut behind us, enclosing us inside a long, empty room. The thirty or so viruses that had filed in alongside us all started looking around in confusion. "What is this?"

"Looks like some kind of renal cyst," I said. "They locked us in."

"I can see that, but—"

"Shhh." Without the light from outside, it took a second for my eyes to adjust. I switched on my halogen headlamp, but the beam wasn't nearly as strong as before, the bulb just bright enough to cast long shadows along the wrinkled outlines of the walls. The other viruses shrank back, huddled in groups away from the door. All casual banter had ceased.

"What's going on?" I whispered.

"Nothing," Astro said, "probably just more scare tactics." But he didn't sound too sure of himself anymore.

"No, man," a voice said behind us. It was the rotavirus I'd seen coming in. "It's different now. I heard they're using NK cells down here."

Astro looked at him. "Dude, don't say that, not even as a joke."

"NK," I said. "What, you mean natural killer cells?"

The rotavirus nodded grimly. "Yeah, for real. Leukocytes brought 'em straight out from the marrow, no lie."

"But we're just small-timers," Astro said. Now he was

starting to sound anxious. "I mean, look at me, I'm not a threat. You know the last time I even *infected* a cell? We're not worth the perforin that it would take to wipe us out!"

"Doesn't matter." The rotavirus shook his head. "Pressure's coming down from on high. New immunity initiative or something. My buddy told me last week NKs came through here and it was just a massacre, man. I'm not kidding—they're *still* mopping up the stains."

"And they're coming here?" I said. "When?"

That was when we heard it—a faint rumbling from outside the room. It was already getting louder, building up, becoming a steady roar that filled the entire space around us.

Astro's voice was just a whisper, realization filling his eyes with dread:

"They're already here."

# TWENTY-SIX ::: HARLAN

By the time I got to the cafeteria for lunch, the whole school was already buzzing about what happened with me and Zooey in gym class. The only good news was that I'd managed to lose Lenny's parents in all the commotion. Maybe they'd gone back to yell at Mr. Cheney some more about their missing son.

Considering how long Lenny and I had been friends, I didn't know that much about his mom and dad. Whether they realized it or not, Lenny spent most of his life just trying to live up to their expectations—which basically meant trying to be like them in every possible way, right down to the color of his socks. And the older he got, the worse it was. Once he told me he'd actually found a timeline that his parents had sketched out for him, mapping his future from high school and college to a series of cutting-edge scientific discoveries. He got as far as "time travel" and "cures cancer," and couldn't read any more.

In the lunch line, I grabbed my tray, a bowl of chili, and a chunk of cornbread, and looked around the cafeteria, searching for an empty table. With Lenny gone, I wasn't sure where to sit.

"Harlan?"

I turned around and saw two sixth-graders—Mark Nichols and Arabinda Choudhary—standing behind me. Mark was holding a coffee can with Lenny's yearbook picture from last year taped to the side of it, along with the words HAVE YOU SEEN ME?

"What's this?"

"We heard Lenny's missing," Mark said. "We're collecting money to hire a private detective."

"*What?*"

"Lenny was, like, a hero to us," Arabinda said. "I seriously never understood Euclid's proof of the infinitude of prime numbers until he explained it to me."

"Yeah." Mark bobbed his head up and down, the lights of the cafeteria beaming off the thick lenses of his glasses. "When we heard he was abducted, we just wanted to do whatever we could to help."

"Guys, he wasn't—"

"We've already raised almost thirty dollars in dona-
tions." Mark shook the jar. "People around here really
care about him, you know? They've really dug deep."

"Just shut up a second, okay? Lenny's not—"

But Mark wasn't listening to me. He and Arabinda
were both staring at something over my shoulder, their
eyes wide in matching expressions of awe.

"Oh, *man*," Mark said. "You think she's actually going
to *eat* all that?"

I turned around and immediately realized what he
was staring at. Zooey was coming out of the line, strug-

gling to carry her lunch tray in front of her. Piled on top of the tray was a metropolitan skyline of cafeteria food. From here, I counted six bowls of chili, an entire loaf of cornbread, two hot dogs, and a soft pretzel, along with three apples, a basket of onion rings, a giant dish of soft-serve ice cream, and at least five cartons of milk. Cutting through the crowd, she found the nearest empty place, set the tray down, unwrapped her plastic spoon, and tried to decide where to start.

"Hey," I said, going over to sit down next to her.

"Oh." She looked at me. "Hey."

"Hungry, huh?"

"*Starving*. I seriously don't know what's gotten into me." She spooned chili onto a piece of cornbread and devoured half of it in one bite, delicately blotting a drop of juice from the corner of her mouth. "I just need to *eat*. My whole body is just screaming, like, *Feed me now*, you know? It's seriously ridiculous, but I don't think I've been this ravenous in my entire life."

I thought about what Lenny had said about her appetite increasing. "Maybe you should take it easy."

"Mmm." Zooey held up one finger, chewed, and swallowed. "Listen, I wanted to tell you, about what happened in gym class . . ."

"It's all right."

"No, it's not," she said, dunking an onion ring into her vanilla soft serve, then taking a big bite. The food seemed to help her focus. "It's *really* not."

I tried not to notice, but I could feel everybody in the cafeteria staring at us. Some of them had their phones out and were taking pictures. Over by the salad bar, I saw Aria standing with a handful of other eighth grade girls. She was just gazing at us with that cold blankness in her eyes, like a mirror that ate the light and reflected back nothing at all.

"Zooey, listen . . . I don't know exactly what's going on here, but—"

Zooey stopped eating and looked at the tray in front of her as if seeing all the food on it for the first time. "Oh no," she said in a small voice, and let out a shaky breath. "This isn't really happening, is it?" All of a sudden, she sounded wrung out and exhausted. "I mean, really, I keep asking myself, nobody can possibly be having this bad of a day, can they? At least some part of it must be all in my head . . . right?"

"Listen," I said, and tried to find a way to put my arm around her without making it seem weird. "It's going to be okay. Everybody has bad days. Just—"

Zooey jerked upward. *"Don't touch me!"*

"Oh, whoa, okay." I reared back, yanking away my arm, startled by the anger in her voice while she sat there with her eyes burning holes in me. Her face was bright red again, but this time it was from pure rage. She looked less like an eighth grade girl and more like one of those primitive statues that we'd studied in non-

Western world history, the ones that early tribal people put out to ward off evil spirits.

*Nice one, Lenny,* I thought. *Was this what you meant to do to Zooey when you went in this morning? Because somehow I doubt it.*

I took in a breath. "Okay, just . . . hold on, all right? There's an explanation for this. Your hormones—"

"Don't you *dare* start talking about hormones to me, understand?"

"Zooey—"

"Just do yourself a favor and quit while you're ahead, Harlan." When she sprang to her feet, her elbows caught the edge of her overloaded lunch tray and flipped the whole thing forward, slopping a tidal wave of chili, corn-bread, and milk across the table and down the front of her shirt. Whirling around, she stormed out of the caf-eteria and disappeared through the exit. The lunchroom had fallen absolutely silent, and for a second the only sound was the hydraulic hiss of the door shutting in her wake.

I got up and went after her.

"Mr. Williams?" It was Mrs. Henry, one of the math teachers, filling her cup with iced tea. "Where do you think you're going?"

"Out." I cut through the doors without a backwards glance, heading past the row of vending machines that stood along the hallway leading back to the office, and looked around the corner and down the hall, to the right and left.

Zooey was nowhere to be seen.

I got out my cell phone and dialed Lenny's number. Straight to voice mail.

"All right, listen up, jerk," I said. "This has gone too far. If you care about Zooey at all, you'll get out of there right now—you understand me?" I waited. "Call me as soon as you get this. I'm serious, Lenny. If you don't stop this . . ." The words broke off, and then I finished the thought: "I don't know if we can be friends anymore. Call me."

I clicked off, and felt somebody coming up behind me.

"Harlan?"

"Look," I said, thinking it must have been one of the teachers. "I know I'm not supposed to make calls during school hours, but . . ."

My voice faded as I looked around, and saw Aria standing there.

"We need to talk," she said.

## TWENTY-SEVEN : : : ZOOEY

I got as far as the front door and realized that I didn't know how I was going to get home.

Usually I rode the bus to school, or Dad dropped me off on his way to work. But right now all I knew was that I couldn't stay back there another second. I needed to change my clothes and get control of myself, if that was even still possible.

After walking out the door, I stood on the front steps with my arms crossed, shivering in the cold, trying to think of one of Martha's rules that could apply to this situation. To my knowledge, she'd never had a moment when she felt like she was losing her mind. I had no idea why I'd reacted the way I had to Harlan, or exactly when I'd lost all control of my feelings, but if I couldn't get it all straightened out by three thirty today, everything was going to be a total disaster.

Looking up, I realized that big fluffy white flakes had begun drifting down out of the sky.

It was starting to snow.

I walked down the steps and past the student and faculty parking lots, bracing myself for the long walk home. I'd forgotten my coat, and I didn't have a pair of boots, mittens, or a hat. At this rate I'd be sicker than ever by the time I got back to my house, but at least I could finish losing my mind in private—assuming that I even made it that far before I had a total psychiatric collapse. If not, no big loss, right, Zooey? What's one more hysterical middle-schooler?

For some reason, I started thinking about the virus that I'd asked Lenny to come up with for the play. He'd never gotten back to me about it. In fact, I hadn't seen him at all today, which was unusual, because I always kind of had the feeling that he was watching me. Not in a creepy way . . . Well, no more than usual.

I was playing it back in my head, stepping off the sidewalk and down the over the curb, when I saw the Prius speeding right toward me, blasting its horn.

I jumped to the right and the car swerved past me, tires squealing, slipping on the new-fallen snow, then stopping and backing up. I saw a man and woman inside, the man behind the wheel, powering down his window.

"Are you all right?" he asked.

I stopped, crossing my arms again to hide the chili stain down the front of my shirt, and looked over at him. He was bald with a long, serious face that I recognized from somewhere. The woman in the passenger seat was holding a crumpled Kleenex in her hands, coddling it between her knees like a cracked egg. I knew I'd seen them before, and then I remembered where—back inside the school, by the gym.

"Yeah," I said. "I'm okay."

"You go to school here, don't you?"

I nodded.

"I'm wondering if you know our son," the man said. "Lenny Cyrus?"

I looked back at them again, and that's when I saw the resemblance—the softness of his mom's face combined with his dad's hard eyes and nose. "You're his parents?"

"That's right," the woman said. "And Lenny, he's . . ." She flicked her eyes at her husband. "Something's happened to him. He's . . . well, he's—"

"He's made a poor choice," Lenny's dad finished for her. "A series of them, actually."

"I heard he went home."

"He's not home," his dad said. "At the moment, we're not sure where he is."

"Did you ask Harlan Williams? He's Lenny's best friend."

"Yes, we know Harlan." Lenny's dad got a sour expression on his face. "He was . . . less than helpful. What's your name?"

"Zooey. Zooey Andrews."

"Zooey . . ." His parents exchanged a look, and Lenny's dad shrugged. "I think Lenny might have mentioned you before. Do you mind if I ask where you're going?"

"Home," I said, and realized they were both staring at me. "I had to leave class. I had an accident at lunch."

"I thought I smelled chili," Lenny's dad said, looking at the stain on my shirt and then trying not to look at it. All things considered, he was about as subtle as his son, which shouldn't have surprised me.

"I'm not feeling the best, and I have to go home and change my clothes."

"Well, then, you certainly shouldn't be out without a jacket," Lenny's mom said. "Get in—at least let us give you a ride."

I opened the back door of the car. The back seat of the Prius was buried under heaps of hardcover textbooks and magazines with titles like the *American Journal of Microbiology*. Any remaining doubt that these two people weren't Lenny's parents went right out the window.

"Just push those aside," Lenny's mother said, reaching around to shove them to the floor. I climbed in and pulled the door shut, fastening my seat belt as I stared out the window at the snowflakes skirling past. As we drove off, I realized that my toes were twitching, my fingertips tapping—even my eyes didn't seem to be able to hold still. Apparently the newest incarnation of Psycho Zooey was due to arrive any second now.

"... where you live?" Lenny's dad was asking from the front seat.

"What?"

"Your address." He sounded impatient, as if now that I couldn't help him find Lenny, he just wanted to get rid of me. "Where do you live?"

"Oh, it's ... down that way. Take a right." I pointed up to the next intersection and saw his eyes watching me from the rearview. "So, how long have you been trying to find Lenny?"

"Since this morning." His dad shook his head. "I'm sure he's fine," he said. "This is his idea of a joke, but it isn't very funny."

Once we reached my street, I showed him where my house was, and I was about to get out when I had one last thought.

"Did you try his cell phone?"

"At least a dozen times," his mother said, and drew in a shaky breath. The damp, wadded Kleenex in her hand was now the size of a marble. "Wherever he is, I just hope he's not in trouble."

## TWENTY-EIGHT ∷ LENNY

"*Dude,*" Astro shouted, "*we're so dead!*"

When the natural killer cells burst into the renal cyst, I knew right away it was going to be a massacre. I heard screaming, and a loud, horribly juicy noise erupted from somewhere in the darkness off to my right with a sudden *SPLAT*, spraying me like the world's biggest water balloon. I glanced back to see a rhinovirus deflating in a stringy puddle of goo. Astro lunged away in the opposite direction like he thought there might be an exit for him, but I could have told him it was a dead end. I could see the whole room from here.

*It's not a renal cyst,* I thought. *It's a death chamber.*

The NKs came in swarms, cutting down through the

inside of the chamber like a giant school of flying piranha. I'd seen them in textbooks and under the microscope, but up close these things were butt-ugly, a dull shade of grayish-green, faceless and featureless except for the gaping holes—what I first took to be their mouths—at the front of their blunt, squashed-looking faces. Unlike the leukocytes, which at least seemed to think individually, these things were stupid, vicious, and hungry. It was middle school all over again.

The viruses never stood a chance. Everywhere I looked, they were screaming, clawing the walls and trying to escape. I heard one of them backing away, trying to hold its nucleic acids inside its capsid, but it was hopeless. A pack of NKs closed in on the rotavirus that had just been talking to us a second earlier, and that was when I realized that openings in the front of the NKs weren't mouths. They ejected a thick stream of granulated fluid on the rotavirus, and its whole body instantly started to shrivel and melt, membranes collapsing while it screamed, reduced to streaks of gelid proteins that wafted away into nothingness.

Viruses were dropping right and left. Astro and I had nowhere to go, which he made even more obvious when he jumped behind me to hide.

"Wait," I shouted at the NKs. "I'm not a virus! I'm just a kid!"

They didn't seem to hear me, and if they did, they didn't care. All around me, the packs of them thickened,

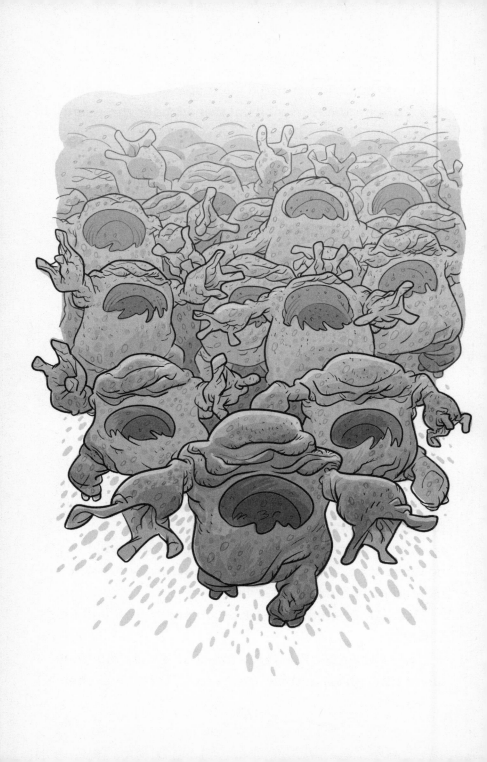

and I realized that Astro and I were the only ones left. It had taken them five seconds to kill almost every virus in the place, and now it was our turn. The holes in the fronts of their faces opened up, and I could actually see the protease that was going to melt our faces—*my* face, right off my skull.

I realized that, to these guys, it didn't matter what I was.

I may have lived like a human being, but I was going to die like a virus.

When the NKs started exploding around us, I didn't re-alize what was happening. At first, I just saw big chunks of protease flying off in every direction, a split second before it would have killed me and Astro. Then another NK blew up, and a dozen more after it, smashing against the walls on either side and then falling to the floor, bro-ken and twitching, oozing clouds of granular goo from the openings in their flattened heads.

"Let's go!" a familiar voice shouted, swooping down through the room and coming in close. "Let's move, peo-ple! Get in there and get dirty!"

Astro shrank back, and then his whole chubby face relaxed into a big relieved smile. "Whoa," he said, in a voice that was even more dazed than usual, "I don't be-lieve it."

"Who—?" I said, and the words broke off as I under-stood what was happening.

"Are you two reprobates ready to evacuate the prem-
ises?" Lug asked, swimming up in front of us. "Or did
you plan on loitering out here indefinitely?"

I stared at him in near disbelief. Since I'd turned him
into a caffeine molecule, Lug's vocabulary had improved,
but he'd also grown somehow even *bigger*—his molecular muscles had muscles on top of *them,* as if he'd spent
the intervening time doing pushups and squat-thrusts
while memorizing a thesaurus. The squadron of steroids
that he'd brought with him circled the renal cyst, wiping
the floor with the last of the NK cells, who still didn't
seem to understand exactly how things had turned on
them so suddenly. They scrambled out through the hole
that Lug's pals had created on their way in.

"Well, what do you say? Ready to go?"

"Yeah," I said, "absolutely."

"Outstanding," Lug said. "Let's move. I've got a proposition for you that I think you'll find extremely provoca-
tive."

"Where are we going?"

"I know a joint not far from here," he said. "Follow
me."

The joint in question was in Zooey's neck—Lug and his
crew led us up the subclavian and detoured through a
capillary bed. The whole place was a boardwalk of junk
DNA along the shores of a lymph node that seemed to
stretch out forever.

"It's a safe rendezvous," he explained as we slipped between the endothelial cells. "Close enough proximity to the BBB, but far enough off the beaten path that not anybody would come poking around."

I looked around the long, desolate expanse of membrane stretching out in front of us with lymphocytes rolling up the shoreline, full of molecules I didn't recognize, crippled viruses and fringe-dwellers. Some of them were bacteria who'd tried to get across the blood-brain barrier and never made it, or just gotten lost along the way. It was a boulevard of broken bugs, microbes that Zooey's body didn't know she had, but weren't worth destroying.

"Dude, thanks for the assist back there," Astro said. "That was extremely cool of you."

"Not a problem." Lug and his small army—twenty or thirty steroids at least—relaxed into their corner of the epithelium. "We heard rumors about NK activity in One Kidney and figured you boys could use some backup."

"So what's this proposition you mentioned?" I asked.

Lug smiled. "Straight to business, huh?" He nodded. "I like that." He settled back and pointed at me. "It's Lenny, right?"

"That's right."

"Maybe you don't know it, but you're stirring up a lot of interest down here right now. Everybody's talking about this mysterious new arrival. Nobody's quite sure what he is." He smiled again, but this time the smile was different—self-aware, almost sly. "All I know is, ever since you worked your magic on me? I feel amazing."

"Thanks," I said. "It was just simple chemistry."

"Humility, huh? I like that. Nice touch, but don't sell yourself short. You're an artist." Lug gestured to the steroids gathered around him. "I want you to do it for all my crew."

I blinked, not sure I was hearing him right. "You want me to turn *all* of you into caffeine molecules?"

"You do that for us, we'll get you through the blood-brain barrier so fast that the neurons won't know what hit them." Lug stepped back, seeing the expression on my face. "I mean, you can do that, right?"

"Yeah, I could, but—"

"So it's no problem?"

"Well, no, but—"

"Then it's settled. You can get started right now."

I saw the steroids already lining up, peeling open their membranes so I could rearrange their atomic structure. I didn't know what it would do to Zooey to have the steroids in her body converted to caffeine molecules, but it couldn't be any worse than all the Diet Coke she drank for breakfast, could it? And getting across the BBB was all that mattered, right?

I nodded and started rolling up my sleeves. "Let's get to work."

# *TWENTY-NINE* : : : *HARLAN*

"I know what's really going on," Aria said. "With Zooey."

"No offense, but I'm pretty sure you don't." We were standing between the vending machines outside the cafeteria, far enough away from the doors so that she didn't have to lower her voice, but I still wanted to shush her. Every PA speaker in the school was two-way, and if there was one thing I'd learned, it was that there were ears everywhere.

"Just listen, okay?" Aria asked. "Zooey's sick." She dropped her voice to a stage whisper. "I think maybe she's on something."

"*On* something?"

Aria nodded. "I haven't actually seen her doing anything, but—"

"Trust me: Zooey's not on drugs."

"You don't know her like I do." Aria bit her lip. "I'm really worried about her, you know?"

"Yeah, well, you didn't seem too concerned a second ago," I said. "Back when she was falling apart back in the lunchroom."

Aria stared at me, looking seriously offended by the accusation. "When I tried to talk to her in the locker room, she went nuclear. Just totally blew up on me in a very messy way. Kind of like she did with you back there, but about a hundred times worse. I learned my lesson."

"I'm sure there's an explanation for it."

"No," Aria said, "it's just Zooey. She thinks she can fix everything herself, like she doesn't need anybody else." She gave a little shrug. "If you didn't know that about her, you don't know much."

"Is there some way we can help her?"

"First things first. We've got a show in less than three hours. At this point I think we have to assume that Zooey's not functioning the way that she's supposed to. We're on our own. Do you understand what I'm saying? *The show must go on.*"

She just stared at me, waiting for a response. There was something that I didn't trust in her eyes. How well did she really know Zooey?

There was only one way to find out for sure.

I turned and started heading for the doors.

"Wait," she said. "Where are you going?"

I didn't look back.

"I'm going to find Zooey," I said.

# *THIRTY* ∶∶∶ *ZOOEY*

*Rule #7: Never be afraid to take a step back.*

It felt weird being back at my house in the middle of a weekday, with nobody else around. Walking through the living room, glancing at the framed pictures on the piano and the ones hanging on the walls, my mind started racing. Memories began flashing through my mind. It wasn't as if I was even *trying* to remember, it was like all these past childhood experiences were just bubbling up, rising to the surface on their own, events that I hadn't thought about in ten years or more.

I realized that I could remember the day we'd moved in, back when I was six and there were moving boxes everywhere. I remembered my first bike, taking the training wheels off, going out in the backyard with my dad to spray-paint it pink, with stenciled lightning bolts on the side. I remembered Mom and Dad arguing about her weekend schedule, and the two of them making up afterward, and how we'd all gone out to dinner at Red Robin. It had been a Saturday afternoon, and I'd ordered macaroni and cheese and a chocolate-covered brownie bites for dessert, and they said it was okay even though I'd already had a large Pepsi with my meal, and our waitress was a blond woman and she was pregnant and she a red vest on, and I—

*I was six years old.*

That was eight years ago.

I could still remember what both my parents had been wearing. It was like they were standing right in front of me. The memory was crystal clear. They all were.

And there were more where that came from. Thousands more. I could hear my parents' voices talking in the front seat when they thought I was asleep, and taste my dad's barbecue sauce, and hear the clink and rattle of him tinkering with the engine of the old Impala that he used to drive to the office. I felt the texture of my mom's red apron, the way it felt different when there was flour spilled on it. I could hear her leaning over my crib when I was too young to even talk, her happy voice in my ear singing that corny old Elton John tune "Your

Song." No matter how far back I looked, the memories just kept going, like stones leading across the water, going all the way back to . . . where? Infancy? Birth? Even before that?

*Next stop, Crazy Town.*

It was almost one o'clock.

I poured myself a glass of Diet Coke and took it up to my bedroom. I switched on the light and stared down at my desk.

I had work to do.

## THIRTY-ONE : : : LENNY

"Hey, kid."

"Hold on a second."

"*Lenny—*"

"What?"

"You can stop now."

I glanced up. "Sorry?" I was still busy switching the steroids into caffeine molecules, with the rest of the line stretching all the way up the capillary bed. For the last twenty minutes I'd been yanking off the atoms of Lug's crew and rearranging them on the nitrogen bindings, and the joints in my fingers were starting to ache, the way they sometimes did when I spent too long at the keyboard. I took a step back to shake off my hands when I realized the line had disappeared.

"Looks like they figured it out for themselves," Lug said, beaming like a proud general over his troops. "Viral learning."

"Now *that's* what I'm talking about," Astro said.

"Wait a second," I said. "The steroids have started converting *themselves* into caffeine molecules?"

"Why not? Is that a problem?"

"Well, theoretically, yes. I mean, if *every* steroid in Zooey's system spontaneously changes into a caffeine molecule . . . ?"

"She'll save a fortune on Diet Coke." Lug shrugged. "Anyway, we've got more pressing matters to discuss." He gestured, waving me underneath the archway of a vessel wall, and pulled out a big sheet of paper, scrolling it out to reveal a detailed diagram of Zooey's brain with different parts labeled. "How much time do you have left?"

I checked the readout inside my face mask. "A little less than two hours."

"You ready to talk about the plan?"

"Whenever you are."

"Good, because we've got a lot to cover." Lug pointed at the diagram, indicating the base of Zooey's brain. "Now there are two main arteries into the brain, here and here. We'll take the CSF through the cerebral aqueduct and come up here, the median eminence of the hypothalamus. Security-wise it's our best bet. I've got a couple of good adrenaline molecules, Twitch and Surge, that can handle crowd control on this end. But once we breach the BBB . . ."—his expression darkened—"things start getting a little dicey. Brain's got all kinds of defense mechanisms to guard against the slightest increase in osmolality in the plasma. If we trip any of the osmoreceptors in the hypothalamus, ADH production is going to go absolutely berserk."

"Sounds like a tough maneuver," I said.

"Oh, that's not even the hard part." He glanced over at me to make sure I was still following him. "Your pal Astro tells me this is an emotional mission, so that means we need to get you into the third ventricle, *here* . . ."—he traced our route along the diagram—"to the limbic system." He looked at me and grinned. "That's where things get *really* tricky."

"Tricky how?"

"How well do you know the terrain up there?"

"I studied the cranial nerves last year in science." I'd actually audited a college-level class on neural anatomy, but now didn't seem like a good time to be trumpeting my academics. "I picked up a few things."

"Good," Lug said. "Then you already know there's a hundred billion cells up there, and the whole area is wired for sound. We're talking millions of electrical signals traveling about three hundred miles an hour, which means they're crossing the entire body in something like a hundredth of a second, giving us zero response time if things go south." He turned back to the diagram. "At the center you've got the pituitary, the master gland, the sympathetic and parasympathetic centers, plus the paraventricular nucleus here, spitting out oxytocin on anything that moves. Basically, the whole thing is one big alarm system. And we've somehow got to move you through all of that without tripping any of these wires, and get up into hypothalamus. And that's not even fig-uring in our exit strategy."

"Exit strategy?"

"You're not exactly sneaking in." Lug waited while I digested this assessment of the situation. "If you haven't already rung every bell in the place, that's definitely go-ing to do it."

"Are you sure it's safe?"

"Oh, yeah. We'll be fine."

"No," I said. "I mean, safe for *her*. Us being up there like that."

Lug just looked at me, then over at Astro, and both of them gave a shrug. "I don't know, chief. It's your rodeo."

I took a step back, trying to get some perspective. The blood-brain barrier was there for a reason. It was Zooey's most critical protection, her last line of defense, and we were about to punch a hole through it. Up till now I'd been swept along by sheer momentum of the operation, but after this, there would be no turning back. What if I did something to her that couldn't be reversed? I needed some advice from somebody even smarter than I was, and that was a pretty short list.

"Hold on," I told Lug. "I need to make a phone call."

Before he could argue, I tapped a button on speed dial, waiting while it rang and rang.

*They won't answer. He's busy. He won't take your call. You made him mad, and now he's just going to ignore you and—*

Then a voice picked up.

"Hello?"

"Dad?" I said. "It's me." I swallowed hard. "It's Lenny."

There was a long pause.

"Dad, can you hear me?"

"Oh, I can hear you just fine, Lenny," he said, and even though the connection wasn't the best, I could hear the coldness running through his voice. "Where are you right now? The mall? Because we've already established that you're certainly not in school."

I sighed. Just the fact that he thought I would ever go to the mall made me realize how little he really knew me. "Dad, listen. I need to ask you something. It's really important."

"Let me ask *you* something first, Lenny. How do you think it makes your mother feel when you put us through something like this? You think it's funny? You think it's all a big laugh?"

"Dad, what are you talking about?" I turned around

and saw Lug and the other molecules jostling around impatiently, eager to get started. "I already proved to you that I made the miniaturization process work, I shrank myself down, and I'm outside the brainstem of Zooey Andrews."

"The Brainstem? What's that, the name of some new video arcade?" There was a rustling noise as he covered the mouthpiece and spoke to my mom. "It's Lenny. He's claims that he's calling from outside the *Brainstem*."

"Dad, listen, okay? This is important. I'm about to go through the blood-brain barrier, and I need to know—"

"Don't waste your breath," Dad said. "Harlan already told us the truth."

"What?"

"He let us in on the joke. You haven't shrunken your-self down to the microscopic level any more than you've flown to the moon." He gave a dry, humorless chuckle that came out more like a snort. "Frankly I can't believe I ever fell for that in the first place. Serves me right for thinking you could do it, I suppose. I won't make that mistake again."

"Dad—"

"I'm only going to say this once, Lenny. Wherever you are, you'd better drop what you're doing and get your rear end back home right now. We are *extremely* disap-pointed in you."

"You . . ." I looked around again at the molecules and vessels, taking in a view of the human body that nobody else in the history of science had ever seen with his own eyes. "You're disappointed?"

"Honestly, what did you expect? When you indulge in this kind of juvenile behavior, it only confirms our decision."

"What decision?"

He cleared his throat. "Your mother and I are sending you to Brixton Academy."

"What? *When?*"

"Immediately after the break. We've already spoken with the dean, and they've made a spot for you starting in January."

"That school's in Connecticut!" I was shouting now, but I didn't care. "When am I going to see Harlan and Zooey?"

"You won't," Dad said. "That's the point. After this little stunt, removing yourself from their influence seems like exactly what you need to apply yourself properly to your studies."

"Apply myself? You don't think that I *apply* myself?"

"I think that's safe to say, yes."

I paused and tried to calm myself down. "When I did this, I thought you'd be proud of me. I thought you'd realize that I've done everything you'd ever wanted me to."

"Lying, skipping school, and pulling infantile pranks isn't exactly living up to your potential," Dad said. "Now, what was so important that you decided to finally call us?"

I held my breath for a second, unable to speak. My heart was thumping hard, and I could feel it throughout my entire body.

"Forget it," I said, and hung up the phone, turning back to Lug and the others, who were crowding closer to me than ever.

"Well?" Lug asked.

I nodded. "Let's go."

## *THIRTY-TWO* : : : *HARLAN*

With the snow blowing and drifting across the road, it took me forty-five minutes to get from school to Zooey's house by bike, not counting the time I got lost in the wrong neighborhood and couldn't find her house. I'd never been over to her subdivision before, and I had to look up her address online—it was a little white two-story gingerbread at the end of the street with a white picket fence and a red, white, and blue mailbox.

Before I could think too hard about the stupidity of this mission, I dumped my bike in her driveway, ran up to the front porch, and hit the doorbell. Nobody answered. I put my ear to the door and listened. Somewhere inside I could hear music playing, the bass booming, turned up loud. I hesitated for a second, trying to decide what to do, but it didn't take me long to make up my mind.

I turned the knob and stepped inside.

It's always weird going in somebody's house for the first time. You never knew what it would smell like, or if they have a dog, or if, like my Uncle Karl's house, there were going to be creepy clown paintings hanging everywhere.

Zooey's house was spotless. I mean, I don't think I've ever seen a house this clean. Everything *gleamed*. The only pictures on the walls were photos of Zooey and her parents. There was a Christmas tree in the living room, decked out with lights and ornaments with a bunch of presents underneath. Over by the fireplace, I saw three stockings hanging from the chimney.

Upstairs, the music kept blasting loud enough to rattle the dishes in the cupboard.

"Zooey?" I shouted. I didn't want to startle her, but there was definitely no way she was going to hear me over the noise. I climbed the stairs, got to the top, and turned the corner, looking down the hallway to the bedroom on the right, where the music was coming from. I walked down the hall, feeling the beat of the bass and drums shaking the walls. The door was open just a crack, and I stopped and looked inside.

It took me a second to believe what I was seeing.

Zooey was standing with her back toward me, leaning over her desk. Spread out in front of her was a scale model of the North Pole set for *Escape Claus*. It was incredibly detailed, big enough to fill the entire desk, complete with little hand-painted miniatures representing each of the actors, and desk lamps to simulate the different types and angles of lighting. From here she looked less like a director working on a play and more like a general getting her troops ready for war. She was busily cutting a hole in the background, singing along with the music.

"Holy crap," I said aloud. "Did you just build that?"

That was when she turned around and saw me.

And screamed.

"It's okay!" I said, holding up my hands. "Zooey, relax, it's just me!"

"*Harlan?*" She stumbled backwards, caught herself, and managed to keep from knocking over the miniature cardboard set. "What are you doing here? How did you get in? How long have you been standing there? Were you spying on me?"

"Zooey, relax. Just calm down, okay?"

She took in a deep breath and blinked at me. "Why are you here?"

"I was worried about you," I said, talking loud enough so she could hear me over the iPod docking station blasting from her dresser. "You mind if I turn this down for a second?"

"What?"

"*Can I turn the music down?*"

She picked up a remote and muted the iPod. The sudden silence rang through the room around us, echoing into empty space, and I could hear us both breathing in the wide-open recesses of it.

"Zooey," I said, "what are you doing?"

"I might ask you the same question."

"I asked you first."

For a second she looked like she was going to argue the point, then shrugged. "I don't know," she said, and another flood of words came bursting out. "I got back to the house and all of a sudden I started to remember things. Like, all this stuff that I hadn't thought of in forever just started popping into my brain."

"Just slow down," I said. "I can't listen that fast."

She managed a slightly bedraggled smile. "Okay, this is the thing, I was on my way home when I got this crazy burst of energy. Then . . . I started remembering things. Like all these details from when I was young, about my mom and dad. I remember my first day of kindergarten, the way I cried until the teachers gave me a set of scented markers to play with and a little boy in purple corduroy pants with an American flag patch on one knee shared his glue with me and—"

"Zooey—"

"It's the craziest thing." When her eyes flashed back to me, I saw how *vivid* they were, all that blue leaping out at me like something inside her was switched up to its maximum brightness. "Harlan, it sounds crazy, but I think I can remember *every single thing* that's ever happened to me in my entire life."

"Zooey, listen—" I drew in a deep breath. "I have to tell you something, okay?"

"Not yet, I'm not finished." She looked back at the miniature set. "See, I figured it out."

"What?"

"Your entrance. The choreography—I've got it all worked out. *I know how to make it work.*"

"That's great," I said.

"It is." She nodded, a little wildly. "It is great. Isn't it?"

"Um, sure." I waited a second, letting it sink in, so she could see that I actually agreed with her. "I still have to tell you something, though."

"Okay. All right. I'm all ears." She just looked at me. Man, those eyes were blue. That was the first time that I realized how pretty she was. How had I not seen it before?

*Whoa.*

I forced myself to get a grip. Was I seriously crushing on Zooey Andrews? And how was Lenny going react if he found out?

"Harlan? What did you want to tell me?"

I took in a deep breath. If I really liked Zooey the way I thought I did, then I owed her the truth, the whole truth, no matter how messed up it was. "Okay, look. This is gonna sound really crazy, and you'll probably want to call the cops on me before I'm done, but just do me a favor and try to let me finish before you dial 911."

She nodded. "Okay. Just make it fast, all right? I have to get back to the school and fix the sets."

"Okay. So, this morning before first period, Lenny and I—"

Downstairs I heard the front door swing open. There was a *thump-thump-thump* of someone stomping the snow off of his boots.

"Zooey?" a man's voice shouted from downstairs. "Whose bike is lying in the middle of our driveway?"

"Oh no." Zooey stared at me. "That's my dad."

I glanced at the clock. It was 1:35. "Isn't he supposed to be at work or something?"

"Not today. He took the afternoon off to come see the play." She turned back to me. "He must have come home to change. You left your bike in my driveway?"

"I didn't know your—"

"Zooey?" Now the voice sounded more urgent, and I could hear boots marching up the stairs: *whomp-whomp-whomp*. I looked around, but there was nowhere to run. I'd heard rumors about Zooey's father, a former U.S. Marine who'd started his own successful home security business, and by all accounts he was not a guy to mess with. Kids at school said that he was the only parent who Shovelhead was afraid of, and the one time that Zooey's dad had gone into gym class to talk to him, Shovelhead looked as if he'd swallowed his tongue.

"Zooey?" He was at the top of the stairs now, rounding the corner and coming down the hallway. "Is there someone up here with you?"

"Get in the closet," Zooey hissed. *"Hurry."* She grabbed me by the forearm, hard, and swung me across the floor, where I somehow kept from falling over, landing on a pile of her clothes inside the closet, just before a shadow fell into the doorway somewhere off to my right.

"What's going on here?" Zooey's dad said. From where I was crouched, holding my breath and peering out, all I could see was the left side of his body, his shoulder and arm as he stood there. "What are you doing home from school? Are you sick?"

"No," Zooey said. "I mean, I was, a little, but now—"

"Whose bicycle did I almost run over in the driveway?"

"It's mine. I mean, it's not really *mine*—I had an accident at school and came home to change. One of my friends loaned me his bike so I could get back here."

"What kind of accident?"

"Nothing big," she said. "I'm fine now."

"Oh. Well . . ." There was a short silence. "Well, you shouldn't have been riding a bike in the snow. And you're lucky I didn't run over it. You would have owed your friend a new bike."

"I think he would have understood."

"You give people too much credit, Zooey. I've always said that."

"I know, Daddy, but—"

"Your Christmas play starts at three o'clock, doesn't it?"

"Three thirty," she said. "But I need to get there early. Is Mom coming?"

"I just talked to her," her father said. "She's on her way."

They both turned and began walking out of the room, and I was just starting to relax when my cell phone went off: "She Blinded Me with Science."

Zooey's dad froze in his tracks, and then, in what felt like slow motion, I saw him turn around to the closet until he was staring right at me.

## THIRTY-THREE ∶∶∶ LENNY

"Come on, man, answer, *answer*." I paced across the long, desolate boardwalk of the epithelium, looking past the waves of dead lymph cells washing up like Styrofoam cups and debris along the vessel's retaining wall, waiting while the phone rang and rang.

"Yo, man," Astro said, "I don't mean to rush you . . ."— lowering his voice, he glanced nervously back at Lug and the group of former steroids, now caffeine molecules, that had started milling restlessly behind us—"but I don't think these dudes are gonna wait around forever."

"I have to get in touch with Harlan." I clicked off and tried again, hoping I could at least leave a message. Lug's plan was risky, and I needed to make sure Zooey was in a safe place when it happened.

*Basically we'll have to short out her temporal lobes, Lug said. Just a little extra electrical current for a second or two, just long enough for you to get out. As long as she's sitting down somewhere, she won't get hurt. She won't even know it happened.*

But how was I supposed to know if she was sitting down or not?

"You want to go or not?" Astro asked.

"Of course I do."

"Then let's *go.* You can call once we're inside."

"Just let me try once more." Looking around, I saw Lug and the others moving back up toward the capillary bed, heading into the bloodstream. "Wait, where are you going?"

Lug glanced back. "Sorry, man, gotta roll. Caffeine's got a half-life of four hours. I want to help you, I seriously do, but we don't have time to wait around forever. You heard the plan. It's now or never."

I checked the clock in my dive mask. Lug wasn't the only one on a deadline. In less than ninety minutes, I was going to start returning to my normal size—if Zooey's body hadn't already tagged me as dangerous enough to hunt down and destroy at all costs.

"All right," I said. "Let's rock."

*:::*

We dove headlong into the brachiocephalic artery and shot upward on a jet of hydrostatic pressure so fast and hard that I felt my eyeballs pop, Lug yelling to me all the way, hollering to make himself heard over the pulsatile roar of Zooey's circulation. "Now listen—when we hit the barrier, let us handle crowd control. We're caffeine molecules now, which means to a nerve cell we look just like adenosine. We'll take out the receptors. You just get yourself into the CSF, and don't look back."

"Where's the—"

"*Heads up!*"

Then I saw it.

We were rocketing straight at the blood-brain barrier, which from here looked like a massive, impenetrable wall closing down on us from above. It was the color of dark volcanic glass, marbled with thousands of tiny blood vessels and millions of motor neurons flickering up and down like chain lightning through its depths. As its shadow fell over my face, I felt my last survival instincts kick into overdrive. Fear clamped down on my throat, and for a second I was sure this was how I was going to die, smashed to pieces against the underside of Zooey's brain.

On reflex, I screamed and groped for the vessel wall in a last-ditch attempt to slow myself down and get turned around, but it was too late. Lug grabbed me and wrapped himself around my body until he'd completely enveloped me in his molecular structure. "Hang on!"

I couldn't let go if I'd wanted to. Alarms were going off now, all along the perimeter, adrenaline spewing from the inside the barrier. Somewhere off in my peripheral vision I was aware of Lug and the other caffeine molecules plowing through ranks of nerve endings, latching on to adenosine receptors and shutting them down. Things had been set into motion now and there was nothing I could do to stop them.

Someone—maybe Astro—was shouting at me to keep going.

I closed my eyes and braced for impact.

And then I was in.

I opened my eyes and looked around.

The sudden burst of turbulence had given way to a smooth expanse of sleek white silence, like the climate-controlled lobby of a very expensive hotel. Listening harder, I heard faint electronic wake-up chimes and whirring noises reverberating across the expanse, all of it surrounded by the steady, reassuring gurgle of cerebrospinal fluid.

My breath caught in my throat.

*I did it. I actually made it up here.*

Up along the walls, hundreds of plasma screens ran in perfect precision, curving with the natural contours of the neural pathways. On all of them, I saw images— high-definition reflections of neural input of Zooey's thoughts, memory, dreams, fears—rippling through densely packed miles of circuitry in a continuous flow of input and fiberoptic processing. I saw a math classroom, a football game, a birthday party, flowers, an iPod, a pretty, dark-haired woman that I realized was Zooey's mother, leaning forward to kiss her good night. The images seemed to go on forever, components and monitors all working flawlessly together. From here, Zooey's brain looked like an Apple store the size of Manhattan.

"Dude," Astro's voice said behind me, "this place is the *bob-omb*."

I jumped in surprise and looked around at him. "I didn't know you were still here."

"What, are you kidding?" Astro reached up with one of his tendrils, groping for the controls underneath a bank of wide-screen monitors. "You think I'd miss this for the world?"

"Don't touch it." I pushed him back. "Don't touch *anything*."

"Chill, bro—I'm cool."

"What happened to the others?"

"What, you mean Lug and the guys?" Astro shook his head. "Lost 'em at the border." He shrugged. "They knew the risks."

I nodded, but something was already starting to feel wrong. "Isn't there supposed to be more security around here?"

"Lug said the hypothalamus was the easiest way through—"

"I know," I said, "but there's *nobody* around."

"Yeah," Astro admitted, "that is weird." He was staring at a monitor showing Zooey's face looking back at her in the bathroom mirror, tweezing an eyebrow. "Hey, you think she gets Cinemax on these things?"

I looked up into the open cathedral of the midbrain, along the white sluiceways that stretched off into the distance, listening to the murmur of CSF flowing around us, a clear and colorless stream of currents that cradled the brain and would carry us wherever we wanted to go. I wished that Lug was still here with his map. "This must lead up to the third ventricle." My voice echoed through the passageways. "If we follow it through the aqueduct . . ."

Then I stopped.

On the big screen in front of me, underneath a suite of processing equipment, I was staring at a three-story-high image of Harlan's face.

He looked terrified.

## THIRTY-FOUR ::: HARLAN

For a second, Zooey's dad just stood there glaring at me with a deep line of puzzlement creasing his forehead. Although I'd never actually seen him in person before, I realized that he looked exactly as I'd expected—a big, broad-shouldered, red-blooded American in his late thirties with a bristly crewcut and a squirmy vein running along the side of his head, ticking in time with the last remaining seconds of my life. He was wearing a suit and tie, and I could smell his aftershave, something inexpensive and basic that he'd probably been wearing since the day he'd met Zooey's mother.

"Who are you?" he asked in a low, ominous voice,

taking a step toward me. "And what in God's name are you doing in my daughter's bedroom closet?"

I held up my hands. "Sir—"

"Daddy," Zooey said, "wait. Don't touch him. He's—he's contagious."

Mr. Andrews stopped and snapped a glance back at her. "He's what?"

"He's got chromoblastomycosis," Zooey said, and blinked in total bewilderment, as if she herself couldn't believe the sheer size of the word that had just popped out of her mouth. "It's a fungal infection of the subcutaneous tissue." Before her dad could say anything, she turned and grabbed a Post-it note from the desk and sketched a diagram, then held it up where her father could see. "See, what typically happens is that an erythematous papule initially appears at the site of inoculation. Although the mycosis slowly spreads, it usually remains localized to the skin and subcutaneous tissue. It's rarely fatal, but it's highly infectious, and . . ."

Mr. Andrews just stared at his daughter as those last words trickled to a halt. I was staring at her too. For a moment we were united, two guys in a state of total confusion.

And then I remembered the code word.

*Freaking Lenny,* I thought, impressed in spite of myself. *You actually made it to her brain.*

After what felt like a very long time, Mr. Andrews turned back to me.

"Is this true?" he asked. "You've got this chromocyto-whatever-it-is?"

"Yes, sir," I said gloomily, looking down at the tips of my shoes. "That's right."

"Then what exactly are you doing here?"

"I wanted to help him," Zooey blurted out, and now she actually looked horrified at what she was saying.

"Zooey, your Christmas play starts very soon. Why in the world would you be back here with—"

"I was the one who gave it to him." She clapped her hands over her mouth and shook her head, but it was already out there, and the vein in Mr. Andrews head looked like it was about to pop.

"What? You? *How?*"

"That's not actually how it happened, sir," I said. "Zooey—"

"That's enough out of you." He turned to her. "I hope you have an explanation for this, missy. And for your sake, it'd better be the truth."

"We were doing a unit on swimming in gym class," Zooey said, "and neither one of us was wearing appropriate footwear by the pool . . ." She shook her head again, harder, her voice coming out in a threadbare whisper. "I don't know why I'm telling you this. I don't even know what I'm saying."

"You. Mr. Fungus." Mr. Andrews pointed at me with a finger the size of a Browning nine-millimeter. "I want you out of my daughter's bedroom and out of this house, right now—do you understand?"

I nodded and stepped out of the closet. Zooey's dad edged backwards and gave me a wide berth as I made a beeline for her bedroom door. For just a second, Zooey made eye contact with me as I turned to leave, and I glimpsed the pale, freaked out, what-the-heck-is-happening expression on her face. I tried to send her a telepathic message, beaming the words into her mind that it was all going to be okay, that her brain hadn't been abducted by aliens or anything like that.

Except that it *was* something like that. Kind of. Almost.

"It's okay," I muttered. "I'm really sorry." I started down the hallway, heading for the stairs, and my phone began ringing again, but before I could answer it, the front door swung open.

I stopped in my tracks and looked up. A tall, dark-haired woman in a business suit and a long coat stepped inside. She was carrying a bouquet of roses and looked at me with a combination of surprise and confusion.

Zooey's mom was home.

We stood there for a second, staring at each other. My phone was still ringing like crazy.

"Hello," I said. "I'm Harlan Williams."

Zooey's mom blinked. "Nice to meet you." She craned her neck to look around behind me. "Is my daughter or my husband home?"

"Yes, ma'am. They both are. I was just leaving."

"That's right." She glanced at her watch and frowned a little. "Today is a school day, isn't it?"

"Yes, it is. It's—it's a long story. I play Santa Claus in your daughter's play, though, and—"

"That's why I'm home early from work." She held up the bouquet of roses. "To see Zooey's play." Then she looked at my phone, which was still ringing like crazy. "You probably ought to answer that, Harlan."

"Yes, ma'am."

"Maybe I'll see you after the performance."

She nodded, and I slipped out the door and down the sidewalk, hitting Talk on the phone as I made my way outside.

"Harlan?" Lenny was shouting. "Can you hear me?"

"What's wrong with you?" I yelled back.

"What?"

"Oh, I don't know, maybe a little thing called chromoblastomycosis?"

"So you got the signal?"

"I got it, all right." I picked up my bike and started wheeling it down into the storm. "What, is that supposed to be funny? Of all the code words in the world, you have to give me . . ."

# THIRTY-FIVE ::: LENNY

"—a chronic *fungal* infection?"

Harlan's voice crackled through the cell phone's earpiece. I'd put him on speakerphone to improve the signal quality, and even with the volume turned down, he sounded like he was ready to rearrange my face. "Seriously, that's what you got? That's the best you can do?"

I stood there in the white inner corridor of the hypothalamus, looking around at the array of screens in front of me, and told myself to be patient. "You know what?" I said. "Just for once, a thank-you would be nice."

"Thank you for what?" he spluttered. "Do you have

any idea how embarrassing that was for Zooey? I mean, forget about me for a second—"

"Oh, and by the way, thanks for telling my dad this whole thing was just a big joke."

"What was I supposed to do, Lenny? Huh?"

"Stick with the plan!" I burst out. "This was the one time that I could actually prove to him that I'd done something that nobody else had ever done, and you ruined everything by telling him it was all just some idiotic prank."

On the big monitor directly in front of me, I was watching Zooey's mom in the entryway of the house. All the other screens were filling with memories, happy images from childhood matching the mood of the moment. Even Astro seemed to get swept up in it. He was staring at the monitor with a big, ridiculous smile on his face, rocking back and forth and humming happily to himself.

"I did it for you," Harlan said.

"Gee, thanks."

"I'm serious, you dope. If your mom and dad really believed you were shrunken down and inside Zooey, they wouldn't have rested until they got you out. They would've pulled her out of school and had her rushed to a hospital and flushed you out of her system. Why did you even have to tell them, anyway?"

I didn't say anything. We both knew the answer to

that one. I couldn't help myself. I'd needed to prove to them—especially Dad—that I could do something like this on my own. Why had I even bothered?

"How much longer is this gonna take?" Harlan snapped.

I glanced at the digital readout and saw that I had slightly less than an hour. "Not long now."

"I hope not, for your sake."

"Look, Harlan—"

"No," he snapped. "Don't, Lenny, okay? Just *don't*. Don't even try to explain."

"Whoa," I said. "I don't know why you're so mad. If anything, I should be the one who's upset."

"Why am I mad?" His voice went up what sounded like another whole octave. "Oh, I don't know, Lenny. Maybe because you *so* don't even care about what you're doing to her?"

"What? That's completely—"

"Okay, first of all, this whole idea of yours was completely idiotic to begin with."

"But it totally worked, didn't it?"

"No," he shouted, "it totally *didn't!*"

"I'm inside, aren't I?"

"Lenny, you still don't get it, do you? That doesn't matter! You don't understand Zooey from the inside any better than you did on the outside!"

For a second I didn't know what to say. The silence

hung between us awkwardly, and then I looked around the various screens reflecting different moments of Zooey's past and present. "Oh yeah?" I said feebly. "Well, that's funny. Because from where I'm standing, it looks like I know everything about her."

"I'm not talking about her freakin' heart rate or her internal core temperature or whatever, you stooge, I'm talking about who she really is!"

"What?" I started looking at the screens again, but all I saw was Zooey's parents standing in the entryway through Zooey's point of view.

"You might be a genius, Lenny, but you can't get to know a person by going inside their body any more than you can change how they feel by going inside their brain. All you did was mess things up and humiliate her and make everything worse. You know why? Because you never think about people's feelings. Just like your parents."

"You . . ." I stood there feeling a hot stab of pain across my chest like a couple of staples down my sternum. It started out as a pinch and got worse, sending a spike of metal up into my throat, and for the first time, my breathing difficulty had nothing to do with the amount of oxygen in the bloodstream. "You . . . seriously believe that?"

"Yeah," he said, "I do."

The line crackled between us for a long moment, neither of us saying anything.

"Okay." It didn't sound like I was the one saying it, but I knew it was. "So then I guess I'll see you around."

"I guess so."

"Harlan, wait—there's something important I need to tell you. It's about how I'm going to get out of Zooey's brain without getting caught. *Harlan?*"

But he was already gone.

"Whoa," Astro said, having overheard the conversation on speaker. "Dude, that was *harsh.*"

I ignored him, still trying to process what happened, telling myself I wasn't going to do anything dumb, like start crying all over Zooey's axons and dendrites. In all the years we'd been friends, Harlan had *never* talked to me like that, even when he was completely exasperated with me, which happened a lot. Even when I'd started a fire in his parents' tool shed by accident, or blacked out the neighborhood with electrical cables, or made half of the school smell like formaldehyde for an entire week, and everybody else had wanted to throttle me within an inch of my life, he'd just shrugged and said, *That's Lenny.*

Not anymore.

"Well, I guess that's what you get," Astro sighed. "These romantic triangles never end well."

"Wait a second." I looked at him. "What are you talking about?"

"A triangle. You know. Three sides? Three points?"

"I meant the romantic part."

"What," Astro said, "are you kidding me? I mean, I might just be a virus, but even I can see that that guy obviously has it for her *bad*."

"That's . . . no." I shook my head. "Harlan knows how I feel about Zooey. He would never—"

"Hey," Astro said, shrugging, "you can keep your delusions. I just call 'em like I see 'em."

I was about to keep arguing the point when I looked up at the screens lining the inner walls of Zooey's brain, at the slipstream of thoughts and ideas pulsing through her consciousness, some of them flickering by at light speed, others lingering long enough that I could make out all kinds of recognizable details.

I was starting to notice a pattern.

Harlan's face was there . . . and there . . . and *there*. All of a sudden it seemed like everywhere I looked, I saw him laughing, talking, walking Zooey to her locker and playing badminton with her in gym class. Harlan wasn't just on Zooey's mind—he was all over her thoughts. The more I looked, the more I saw him. And the more I saw, the less I liked.

Something inside of me went cold. According to the digital display, I had exactly sixty minutes left. I turned and started heading for the CSF flow.

"Wait a second," Astro said. "Where are we going now?"

"To the hippocampus," I said. "It's time to finish what I started."

## *THIRTY-SIX* ∶∶∶ *ZOOEY*

"Be careful," Dad was saying. "I think she's contagious."

"What?" My mom stepped back and stared into my eyes. "Zooey, honey, are you sick?"

"No, it's nothing, Mom," I said. "Just a misunderstanding."

Dad shot me a confused glance, but I barely noticed. A headache had already started forming behind my eyes, a real skull-popper, like a swarm of metal shavings drawn to a magnet, and that dizziness that I'd felt earlier, on the way to gym class, came back with a vengeance. Also, I was getting hot again—except this time, it was chills and hot flashes, one after another. My stomach, still holding the chili and cornbread I'd eaten at lunch, began to tremble and quake.

I looked around. Harlan had taken the golden opportunity to slip out the door, leaving Dad looking more confused than ever.

*If you think you're confused,* I wanted to say, *try looking at it from my point of view.*

A lot of really weird things had happened, but nothing had prepared me for the feeling of somebody else's words coming out of my mouth. My lips had opened with no idea what I was going to say, and the words had just been there, something about a fungus whose name I couldn't even remember anymore, but at the time I'd just stood there reciting scientific facts like . . .

*Lenny.*

"Zooey?" my mom was saying from somewhere far away. She was holding my hand, which meant that she couldn't be too far, and when I concentrated I was able to bring myself back to reality again. "It's almost two o'clock. Shouldn't we be heading back over to the school?"

"Yeah, totally." I was feeling really dizzy now, and I should have just sat down for a second, but there was too much to do. *Rule #9: Never walk into a meeting without knowing how you're going to walk out of it.* I glanced at the keys to the Jeep where she'd set them down on the table next to the door. "Can we take your car?"

"If it's all right with your father."

"Fine with me," Dad said.

"But we have to go right now." I took a step and stumbled, reaching out to catch myself and tumbling through thin air . . .

. . . and landing in total blackness.

## THIRTY-SEVEN ::: HARLAN

The snow was starting to slow down, and I was half a block away from Lenny's house, biking up the sidewalk with my hair caked in snow, when I realized it was already after two. Barring a miracle, there was no way I could get back to school in time to change into my costume before the curtain went up.

But I had to do this. I needed to tell the truth.

I dumped my bike on the lawn, ran up the front steps, and rang the doorbell. A moment later, Lenny's dad's face appeared in the front window. When he saw it was me, he flipped the latch and opened the door.

"Harlan?"

"I need to talk to you," I said.

"Haven't you wasted enough of our time for one day?"

"It's important."

He stood there for a moment as if he wasn't sure he wanted me in his house, then finally stepped aside. "Well, don't just stand there."

I stepped inside the cluttered entryway and down the hall, past floor-to-ceiling bookshelves. Lenny's house was full of books, to the point where they actually seemed to be holding up the roof. You had to walk around piles and boxes of them just to get wherever you were going, and when I was younger I remember thinking that if I pulled out the wrong one, it would bring everything crashing down around me. It was all familiar from a thousand different visits, but it felt different now. The tension made the air feel thick and stale.

In the kitchen, Lenny's mom was sitting at the table with a cup of tea. She stood up when she saw me coming, and both parents were staring at me now, frozen in their tracks, waiting for me to say something.

"He's inside Zooey Andrews," I said.

They both blinked, and his dad frowned. "Who?"

"Lenny was telling the truth the first time. He really did shrink himself down to the size of a molecule, and he's been inside her body for the past five hours."

"Harlan, please"—his dad held up his hands wearily—"that's enough. It's not funny anymore, if it ever was."

"I totally agree," I said. "It's about the most pathetic thing I can think of. But it's true."

"And you actually expect us to believe that?"

"Yeah," I said. "I do."

Lenny's mom and dad just looked at me. I couldn't tell what they were thinking, and at the moment, I didn't care. I'd done what I'd come here to do, tell them the truth, and the fact that they were too stubborn or proud to believe it only made me angrier. "If either one of you had ever bothered to actually take this seriously and listen to him, none of this have happened."

"*Excuse* me?" his mother said.

"Lenny's had a crush on Zooey for years," I said. "*Years*. Since third grade, when she saved him from getting beat up on the playground, he's talked about her nonstop until even I was sick of hearing about it. But you guys . . . you're his parents. You're supposed to care about stuff like this. If you weren't too busy, I don't know . . . winning the stupid Nobel Prize or whatever—"

"I beg your pardon?" Lenny's dad said.

"Was it worth it?" I waved one arm at the bookshelves that lined the walls around them, loaded and sagging with hundreds of textbooks, the framed certificates and awards on the walls, the half-finished experiments and diagrams spread around every surface. "All that time you guys just sat there obsessed with your research and told him to just be himself or whatever? Was it worth the tradeoff?"

"We *did* listen," his mom said. "We told him—"

"You told him not to worry about it. That's exactly

what you said. Just stay cool and be yourself. That's like the worst advice you could ever give a kid. I mean, seriously, just once did either of you ever stop and listen to what he was saying?"

"Of course we did," she said.

"You know what? Forget it." I threw up my hands. "You guys want to know where Lenny is? Now you know. Believe it if you want to, or don't—I don't really care. The fact is that he found a way to make himself really small, and he went where he thought he had to go to fix things, and all he did was make it worse."

Lenny's dad glanced at his mother, and when he spoke again, his voice was quieter, almost unsure of itself. "He called me a little while ago and told me that he was outside her brainstem," he said. "He swore that he was telling the truth."

"But you didn't believe him."

"No."

"Why did he call?"

"He said he had a question. Something really important that he needed to ask."

"What was the question?"

Lenny's dad shook his head. "I don't know. He—he hung up before I could find out." His eyes flicked over to Lenny's mom again. "He was upset. We'd just told him that we were sending him to Brixton Academy after winter break, and—"

"You're sending him to Brixton?" I felt the last of my

patience drain away, and I turned to go. "You guys are really unbelievable, you know that?"

His mom jumped out of her chair.

"Harlan, wait."

But I didn't stop. I walked out, got back on my bike, and started heading to school, double-time.

Lenny wasn't the only one with a schedule to keep.

# THIRTY-EIGHT ::: LENNY

We were floating down the third ventricle, close enough to Zooey's hippocampus that I could actually feel the increased heat from what I guessed had to be the dentate gyrus, when I realized that something was wrong. Astro must have sensed it too, because we both stopped moving at the same time.

"You hear that?" I whispered.

"What?" He cocked his head and listened. "I don't hear anything."

"Exactly." From deep inside the limbic system, the soft, continuous whir of neurogenesis, the sound of new neurons being formed—the reassuring white noise that I'd been aware of from the moment we'd passed through the blood-brain barrier—had fallen utterly silent. It was like standing in middle of a factory that had suddenly stopped production. "It's too quiet."

"What's going on?" Astro asked.

"I have no idea, but . . ."

"Is it, like, really hot in here?"

"Definitely."

"So where is everybody?" He stared at me, waiting. "Where are all the neurons?"

"I'm not sure," I said, not liking the way it sounded. Ever since we'd crossed over the hypothalamus, this whole process had been way too easy. It was like something else had arrived here first and started shutting down electrical activity in the brain, circumventing Zooey's defense systems and taking down the alarms before we'd even tripped them. And now this sudden rush of heat, with the temperature spiking higher than anything I'd felt in the rest of Zooey's body, left me with an increasing feeling of unease, as if I were trapped inside an elevator that had just shuddered to a halt and could—at any second—decide to go plummeting downward.

"Uh, dude?" Astro said. "You might want to take a look at this."

"What?"

"See for yourself." He was staring down at the river of cerebrospinal fluid that had carried us this far up the third ventricle. But the CSF wasn't clear and colorless

like before. Instead, it had begun to turn thick and yellow, with streaks and threads of brownish red running through in its lower depths. It looked like a badly polluted stream outside some ruined industrial city.

"What is that?"

I stared down, unable to speak or move. There was something solid floating in the CSF as it rolled past us. After a second I realized what it was—the corpse of a white blood cell, floating belly-up with its eyes wide open and its mouth gaping like a mackerel's. I heard Astro make a shocked noise, not quite a gasp or a grunt, but something in between, and he cast an anxious glance around to look farther up the ventricle.

"Oh, man," Astro said. "Did you see that?"

I saw. Immediately upriver, the CSF stream was absolutely littered with dead leukocytes and neurons. Their corpses filled the ventricle with a sickish sweet smell, like the bottom of a pile of rotting leaves.

"What could do that?" I asked. "A virus?"

"Uh-uh." Astro shook his head. "No virus that I've ever seen. Zooey's up on all her shots, and believe me, I checked. What about that fungus you were talking about?"

"No, that was just a code word. And anyway, it wouldn't look like this."

"So . . . what is it then?"

"Do I look like a neurologist to you?"

"I dunno," Astro said. "What's a urologist?"

"Forget it." I watched the flotilla of dead nerve cells and white blood cells clogging the CSF flow. "This almost looks more like a meningeal inflammation, or some kind of . . ."

"What?"

"Bacteria."

"No way." Astro was peering down into the infected CSF, trying to get a closer look at it. "Those bugs downstairs couldn't get up if they wanted to."

"Unless they came through when we did," I said. "But how would they get in to start with?"

"I don't know," Astro said, bending down so close that his membrane was almost touching the CSF, "but from the look of this stuff, I think it's—"

That was as far as he got before something reached up from out of the fluid and yanked him in.

# THIRTY-NINE : : : ZOOEY

When I opened my eyes, I was lying on the floor with Mom and Dad both bent over me, looking worried.

"Whoa," I said woozily, staring up at the ceiling. "That's some sun, huh?"

My mom put her hand on my forehead. "Honey, you're burning up!"

"It's that fungus, isn't it?" Dad asked. "I knew it. That cytoplasmic whatever it was."

"Fungus?" Mom glanced at him. "What fungus?"

"Dad, no." I pushed myself up on my elbows and tried to clear my head. "There is no fungus."

"So you lied to me?"

"Honey, for Pete's sake," Mom said. "She probably

doesn't even know what she's saying."

*If you only knew,* I thought blearily. "You're right, Mom. But first we need to get to school."

"School?"

"The play starts in a half-hour."

"Zooey, honey, I'm sure it does, but you're sick. You can hardly stand up."

I turned to my dad, then back to my mother. They both knew what this afternoon meant to me. They'd watched me pour hundreds of hours into the script, set design, and rehearsals, and they knew what was at stake.

"Please, guys. We have to go."

"I'm sorry," Dad said, "but your mom's right. You're in no condition to go anywhere. I'll call the school."

"And tell them what? To postpone the play?" I flashed to the auditorium, where the cast and crew would already be setting up rows of chairs, where Monica Sanossian and Della Marlowe were already putting makeup on the actors. "That's impossible. They need me there."

"Zooey," my dad began, but didn't say anything else. Neither he nor my mother seemed to know how to respond. Some part of me must have expected this, because the plan jumped into my mind fully formed, ready to execute. I felt one last burst of energy, just enough to get me through what I had to do next.

"Okay," I said. "I can't believe you're making me do this."

"Honey—"

I grabbed Mom's keys from the table by the door. "You know where to find me."

Before either of them could say anything, I ran out of the house to the driveway, climbed into the Jeep, and managed to wiggle the keys in the ignition. The dashboard lights came on and my mom's Michael Bublé CD started playing on the stereo, but the engine refused to start.

"Come on, come *on*." I looked up to see my mom and dad coming out of the house after me and tried again, but I couldn't get the motor running. Was she out of gas? How could it be, if she had just driven home?

"Zooey Andrews," my dad was saying, from the other side of the windshield. "Young lady, what on earth do you think you're doing?" Now he was close enough to reach for the door handle on the driver's side. "You're fourteen years old. You don't know how to drive a car."

"I'll figure it out," I mumbled.

"Get out of there right now."

"Drive me to school."

"Absolutely not."

"Dad, drive me to school right now, or I'll drive my-self." *Or die trying,* I thought. In my current condition, it didn't seem so far-fetched.

My dad and mom exchanged a glance, and then he turned back to me. "Get in the back seat."

"Dad, thank you," I said, crawling into the back. "I swear, I'd kiss you if I weren't so sick."

He didn't say anything, just got behind the wheel while Mom climbed in the passenger seat. Michael Bublé was still blaring from the speakers, singing about how he just hadn't met me yet. Mom switched him off and sat there staring back at me as if she were waiting for me to pass out again. The heater in the Jeep started blowing warm air back. I felt myself fading in and out, reality wavering around the edges like a mirage in the desert. That was when I heard the voice.

*Zooey.*

"Huh?" Sitting up, I looked at the radio dial, but the voice wasn't coming from the speakers. It had an echoey, reverberating familiarity, as if somehow it was using my own eardrums as an amplifier.

*It's me. It's Lenny. I'm inside your head.*

"What?" I said, startled. "I don't—" I put my finger in my ear and wiggled it around. "What is this?"

*Just listen. You need to get to a hospital right away. Something's wrong with you. You're really sick.*

"Amazing," I muttered. "Did you just figure that out? You really are a genius."

We came around the next corner, the rear tires sliding over the fresh-packed snow, slipping a little, fishtailing before they caught traction.

Up ahead, I saw the school.

## FORTY ::: HARLAN

My cell phone rang three more times on my way back, "She Blinded Me with Science," over and over, until I finally just switched it off. If I never heard that song again, I'd be okay with it.

When I got back to school, classes were already letting out, but most of the kids weren't leaving. They were headed to the auditorium for the play.

In the guest parking lot, I saw a black Jeep, the one that Zooey's mom had parked in the driveway when she'd gotten home, sitting in front of the gymnasium.

*She's here,* I thought. *She made it back.*

I jammed my bike in the rack down below and ran for

the gymnasium entrance, grabbed the door, and yanked on it, but it didn't open.

"Well, would you look at this," a familiar voice said from the other side of the glass. "You know, Mr. Williams, I believe this may be the first time I've ever seen you trying to get *into* gym."

I didn't need to look closely to know that the voice belonged to Shovelhead. He was standing there on the other side of the door in his running shorts and T-shirt with a big grin on his face, holding the door shut. Watching him, I had an absolutely terrifying vision of Mick Mason twenty years down the road in this same position, intimidating and bullying whole generations of kids into a lifelong fear of physical fitness.

He opened the door just enough to talk through it, but when I reached for the handle, he held on to it tightly.

"What's wrong—you leave your deodorant in your locker?"

"Seriously, Shovel—" I stopped myself just in time. "Mr. Shoenwald. Please, just let me in. I'm in the play. I need to get into costume. I'm on in twenty minutes."

He shook his head. "First things first, Williams. Like, for example, I think you need to go talk to Mr. Cheney. You can explain why you were acting like a complete lunatic in gym today, and then why both of you left school without permission."

"Please," I said. I peered back through the gap in the

door, into the hallway, catching a glimpse of the long line of students waiting to get inside the auditorium. "I can explain it all later. Right now, I really need to get in."

"Sorry, Shakespeare. Rules are rules. You go to the office, then come back and we'll talk." He started to pull the door shut again, and I grabbed it with both hands and yanked as hard as I could.

Shovelhead let out a startled grunt as the door slipped from his grasp and flew the rest of the way open. Before he could stop me, I ducked under his big hairy arm and ran down the hall, sprinting past the drinking fountain and around the corner.

"Hey!" he shouted. "What do you think you're doing! Get back here!"

I ran faster. The kids waiting in line all looked around as I ran past them and cut across the lobby area, into the gym. I could already hear the audience inside, settling into their seats, and through the crowd, I caught a glimpse of a girl dressed in red with her back to me, taking tickets, shaking hands and smiling.

"Zooey!" I shouted.

But it wasn't Zooey.

It was Aria.

## FORTY-ONE : : : LENNY

On first glance, the thing that came slithering out of Zooey's CSF looked like a combination of a giant centipede and something out of the *Alien* movies.

I'd never seen anything like it under the microscope. It scurried up the wall of the ventricle in front of me with what was left of Astro still clamped in its mouth, turned around, and clung there, gazing back at me with a greedy, eager appetite. Its facial features were coming into focus now: narrow beady eyes and a twisted grin.

"Hasn't anyone ever told you that it's impolite to stare?" it asked with a sneer.

"What are you?" I asked.

The thing stopped and frowned at me. "What's that?"

"How did you get in here?"

The thing's grin widened, showing long rows of tiny, layered teeth that came together like a zipper. "That's not an easy question to answer," it said. "I've been on the road a long time. You wouldn't happen to know where we could get something to eat, do you?"

"'We'?"

"Well, yes. I never travel alone."

Off to my right there was a rippling sound, and I looked down and saw that the cerebrospinal fluid was filled with whole colonies of organisms identical to the one in front of me, infesting the entire ventricle and spreading out through the meninges in all directions. Now the sluggish yellow fluid and the dead white blood cells and neurons all made sense. Whatever this thing was in Zooey's body, she didn't have any kind of natural defense against it, zero immunity, because nothing like this had ever been inside of her before.

"How did you get in?"

"I might ask you the same question."

I shook my head. "I'm not the one making her sick."

"Oh, I'm not just making her sick, Einstein. I'm killing her. Thanks to you."

"*What?*"

"You and your buddies left the door wide open in the blood-brain barrier," it said, with sickening smoothness. "We just slipped right through. It was easy."

"How did you get in her system to begin with?"

"Always asking questions, aren't you?" it said, and all the humor fell out of its voice, leaving it sounding low and nasty. "Well, if I had to generalize, I guess you might say our most common vector of infection is bad clams."

"You're . . ." Then I recognized it. "Vibrio vulnificus."

"Nicely done," it said drily. "I'm impressed. Too bad it won't do you any good. Or her."

"I still don't understand how you got in. She's allergic to shellfish. She'd never eat you."

"Not on purpose, maybe."

"But then how—"

"Look around you. The world's a dirty place. And it sure isn't getting any cleaner up here."

"Yeah, but—"

I stopped and looked up. One by one, the monitor screens that lined the walls of the third ventricle were shorting out, cutting over to static for a second and then going completely blank, burying this entire part of the brain in darkness. It was getting hotter in here by the second. Flickering skeins of electrical current sparked and leapt erratically through the synapses around me, and way off in the distance I could feel the faint, juddering thump-thump of Zooey's pulse as it became more irregular.

"Looks like we're really heating up the joint now," the vibrio chortled, and now its grin looked almost demonic. "The immediate forecast doesn't look good."

"Leave her alone."

"Too late for that. We're everywhere."

I checked the digital readout in my dive mask and saw that it was down to eighteen minutes and counting before I started reverting back to normal size.

Then the lights went out.

# FORTY-TWO : : : HARLAN

"Aria?" I ran up to her. "Where's Zooey?"

Aria stared at me, the smile disappearing from her face. "Harlan, where have you been? You were supposed to be in costume and makeup twenty minutes ago."

"I need to find Zooey."

"She's sick. She's not coming."

"No." I shook my head. "She's here somewhere. Her parents' Jeep is parked out front."

"What? Where . . . ?" She looked genuinely shocked. "That's not possible."

"Why?" I looked at her. "Aria, what's going on?"

"Never mind, just go." She shoved me sideways through the door, into the auditorium. I stumbled inside and looked around. Most of the front rows were already occupied, and the remaining empty seats were filling up fast with students, faculty, parents, and friends, all rustling around, waiting for things to get started.

I made my way behind the light and sound board, where Jimmy Colton was making last-minute adjustments to a hundred different knobs and dials, heading into the door that led back to the dressing rooms behind the stage, and that was where I found her.

"Zooey?"

She was leaning against the wall next to a rack of costumes with her parents standing on either side of her, looking worried. Right away I could see why. Zooey's face was pale with blotches of red in her cheeks, and beads of sweat gleaming along her forehead and upper lip. When she saw me, she raised one hand and tried to smile.

"Hey, Harlan." Her voice was a foggy croak. "Ready to be a star?"

"Zooey—"

"Better get your costume on. We're about to start."

"Zooey, no. You need to sit down."

"*Rule number ten. Pain is for the weak.*" She reached out toward me, took my shoulders, and turned me around. "Now listen. Are you listening?"

"Yeah, but—"

"This . . . is what I want you to do. When you first

come out . . . you're going to come busting out through the back of the set."

"What?"

"Just break through the canvas behind the sleigh. Tear it down."

"What about the other performances?"

She shook her head. "We can fix it afterward. Now go get changed."

I flashed a glance at her parents, but neither of them seemed remotely concerned about me destroying the set that it had taken Zooey and her volunteers several weeks to build.

"Zooey, look, I just want to say—"

"Later, okay?"

Out in the auditorium, I could hear the audience starting to go quiet as the houselights dimmed. That snapped me out of it. I took two steps backwards, spun around, and ran to the dressing room. I yanked the curtain shut behind me and grabbed my costume, then rammed my legs into the lower part of the suit and swung the upper part up over my shoulders. I zipped it up, jerking the headpiece on and cinching it tight. I grabbed the boots and finally the mittens with the long crooked fingers sewn into them. It had to be a record for the fastest anybody had ever put this thing on. In the mirror, the zombie Santa leered grotesquely back at me. *Eat your heart out, Ryan Forrester.*

That was when I heard voices from the other side of the room, behind the curtain.

"She's not supposed to be here," Aria was saying. "You told me you took care of it."

"I did," a boy's voice said. "I mean . . . I put that stuff in her soda this morning like you said."

"How much did you use?"

"I dunno, a lot, I guess. All of it?"

"Then how come she's still here?" Aria hissed.

"She's sick, isn't she?" the guy asked. "I mean, did you see her out there? She looks like—"

I stepped forward, reached out with one of the clawed mittens, and ripped the curtain back. Aria and Mick turned around and stared at me, and for a second, Mick looked like he was going to scream. Any remaining threat that he might've posed instantly disappeared. I guess that was what happened when you saw the toughest kid in school wet his pants a little.

"What happened to Zooey?" I stared at them, feeling a combination of anger and disbelief surging through me. "What did you *do* to her?"

Mick glared at me, scrambling to recover. "Nothing, jack-bag. None of your business."

"I heard what you said." All of a sudden I felt the details click—how sick Zooey was, how closely Aria had been watching her throughout the day. "You put something in her soda," I said to Aria. "You were really that jealous of her?"

"Jealous of who?" a voice asked from the doorway.

We all looked around and saw Zooey teetering inside, clutching the door frame to keep herself upright. Her dad was hanging on to her shoulder, holding her back, but Zooey somehow slipped free of him and took another crooked step into the room. Somewhere in the distance, out in the auditorium, I could hear the applause trailing away to silence. A microphone let out a squawk of feedback, and then I heard Mr. Cheney talking to the audience, welcoming them to Cosgrove's annual holiday musical.

"Zooey," Aria said. "You look awful. Are you sure—"

"Stop it, Aria," Zooey croaked, and turned back to me. "Harlan?"

"These guys made you sick," I told her. "Mick stuck something in your Diet Coke this morning."

Zooey's mom let out a gasp, and her dad stared at Mick and Aria, his face turning red. Of the three of them, Zooey herself was the only one who didn't look especially surprised.

"Wait," Zooey said to Aria. "So this morning, when you were talking to Mick . . ."

She didn't finish the thought, just let it trail away. Meanwhile, from out on stage, I heard the first opening notes of the piano score tinkling out, the lights coming up on the North Pole set, as the chorus of elves and reindeer came on stage, singing the opening number.

> *The story you're about to see*
> *Won't light up your Christmas tree*
> *It's a fable dark and fearful*
> *So prepare to get an earful*
> *This year Santa's not so cheerful . . .*

"Forget this. I'm out of here," Mick Mason said, backing up. "You can't prove that I had anything to do with this. I'm gone."

"I need to be out there too." Aria's eyes flashed toward the stage. "Zooey, my cue—"

"Get back here," I said. "Both of you."

"Can it, Williams," Mick snarled. "You think I'm scared of you or your wussy friend?"

I reached out to grab his arm, yanking him back, but my claw-mittens didn't give me the grip I needed. Mick squirmed free, whirled around, and swung, and I ducked, dodging his right fist—but not the left. It went off like a firecracker against my face. My vision on that side went red and then blacked out completely as the lid began to swell shut. My zombie Santa mask hadn't provided any kind of protection whatsoever.

"Harlan," Zooey was saying, from somewhere behind a red layer of pain. "Are you okay?"

"Yeah, I'm fine." Through my good eye, I saw Mick turning to go, and something fell out of his pocket. It was a plastic disk, round and flat like miniature frisbee, and it rolled past Mick's feet in a lazy semicircle, where it finally came to rest at the feet of Zooey's parents.

"It's a petrie dish," Zooey's dad said, picking it up and shoving it in Mick's face. "Is this what you poisoned my daughter with?"

"That's . . . not mine," Mick said uneasily. "I don't know how that got there."

Zooey blinked and looked at it with a slight puzzled frown. She turned to Mick and then finally looked up at Aria, who was regarding her with a stare so cold that it was hard to imagine how they'd ever been able to stand in the same room together.

"Aria . . . ?" Zooey said.

Aria crossed her arms. "You've got a choice, Zooey. Either let me go out on stage and start, or keep me here and ruin your big premiere. What's it going to be?"

Zooey's mouth opened in an attempt to respond.

Her knees buckled, and she collapsed.

## FORTY-THREE : : : LENNY

I reached up and fumbled for the headlamp for a few seconds before realizing I must have lost it somewhere on the way through the blood-brain barrier. In the sauna-hot darkness all around me, I could hear slithering noises, things moving on all sides, coiling and sliding off the sticky surfaces. The only light came from the brief, seizure-inducing flickers of malfunctioning neurons as they arced across the ventricle, showing split-second flashes here and there, like heat lightning.

The whole limbic system was covered in bacteria.

Something grabbed my hand, and I almost screamed.

"Dude," a voice hissed, "it's me."

"Astro?" I turned in the direction of the voice. "I thought you were dead."

"Are you kidding me? I'm a virus, bro. I can survive a nuclear bomb. But you . . ." He looked worried. "You gotta get out of here, now."

"I can't—"

"Just listen. The whole system's going down fast. If you can find a way out, you take it, understand?"

"What about Zooey?"

"Forget it, man. There's nothing you can do."

"What about her heart?"

"Her *heart?*" Astro made a spluttering noise like he couldn't believe what he was hearing. "Believe me, dude, her heart's the last place you want to be right now."

"If I can get down there—"

"Listen," he said, "you hear that?" He stopped just long enough that I could hear the irregular, speeded-up thumping noise that echoed up from somewhere far below. It sounded like a bunch of sneakers in a washing machine. "She's going into v-fib."

"What?"

"Ventricular fibrillation. Cardiac muscle's having seizures. In five minutes the whole thing's going to go blooey. You'll never make it out in time."

"How do I get down there?" I asked.

*"Did you hear a word I just said?"*

I swung around and reached out with both hands in the direction of Astro's voice, grabbing handfuls of soggy membrane. "Get me down there, now."

# FORTY-FOUR ::: HARLAN

"Zooey?"

Somewhere far away her parents were yelling to call an ambulance, but I barely heard them. I got down on my knees next to her and felt the side of her neck for her pulse. I could feel it, but it was all over the place, too fast and too slow at the same time. Her eyes were half open, and the corner of her mouth was bleeding from where she'd hit the floor when she'd fallen. I couldn't tell if she was breathing or not. The heat was pouring off of her in waves like an oven that somebody had left open.

"Hey, Zooey," I said. "It's Harlan. Listen to me, all right? You're gonna be okay. Everything's cool, you're gonna be fine."

Zooey didn't move.

*Hey, Lenny,* I thought, *if you're in there, pal, I could use a little help here.*

# FORTY-FIVE ::: LENNY

By the time Astro and I shot back down to the heart, it was already shaking so hard that I could hardly tell where we were, even if we had been able to see where we were going. The world was a red blur, an earthquake, its epicenter directly in front of us. Astro got as far as the aorta and turned back.

"Good luck in there!" he shouted.

"Wait—I thought you were coming with me!"

"I'm crazy, but I'm not stupid!"

"I thought you said you could live anywhere!"

"I was exaggerating! I could never live here!"

"But—"

"Go!"

I turned and started swimming as hard as I could against the current of blood flowing out of the aorta, kicking with all my strength, pushing with my arms until I was inside what looked like a slick cave of pulsating tissue, all equilibrium gone. *BOOM!* Before I could get my bearings or even look around, I was careening forward

again, then lapsing backwards against the muscle wall, my ears still ringing from the massive, irregular cannon-fire of random contractions as they echoed through the chambers around me. The whole heart jerked, twitched, and seemed to jump underneath my feet, throwing me off-balance again so that I was sprawled out face-first on the salty-slick floor of the atrium. My dive mask cracked and everything went blurry. As my vision cleared I saw blood cells spilling in around me in a frantic mob, look-ing more like they were in search of a way out than any-thing else.

"You!" one of them shouted. "Freeze, right there!"

Somewhere, distantly, I thought I heard my phone ringing. I realized the sound was coming from my skull. Things were losing clarity, getting hazy around the edges, and this time it wasn't from the cracked mask. My brain, which normally worked fine even under stressful situa-tions, was starting to short circuit, and that was when I realized that I wasn't getting enough oxygen anymore. I was going to suffocate down here, if I wasn't knocked to pieces first.

"You're the punk from the hypothalamus," one of the leukocytes snarled. "You're the one who started all this!"

"Wait, I can explain—"

I was wasting my breath, and I didn't have much left. The muscle wall rammed into me again, Zooey's heart going through its final, spastic kicks, and I realized that this was where it was going to end for both of us.

Unless I did something right now.

Thrusting my head forward, I shoved my way into the rubbery clam-shaped opening of the bicuspid valve. It was tight, but I kept kicking forward, working my shoulders through, pushing, squeezing, almost there—and suddenly felt the horrible, sucking mouth of the valve clamp down around my waist.

*Oh no.*

Panic grabbed me by the throat and pinched my airway shut, cutting off the remaining flow of oxygen from the tank. That's when it hit me. I couldn't breathe. I couldn't move. I was stuck halfway through this stupid valve with its individual muscle fibers crushing my hips and spine.

*Not cool. No way. This. Isn't. Happening.*

I thought about Zooey, what I'd done to her, and what I had to do to save her.

*Get through. Just do it. Get through.*

The valve kept tightening, squeezing my insides to jelly. In a second I was going to black out and it would be all over.

*Do it.*

With a final burst of near-hysteria, I yanked myself through. All at once I was in the left ventricle, my arms and legs flailing freely in the turbulence.

It was total chaos. Everything around me was shaking so hard that my vision was blurring around the edges. The momentary relief I'd felt getting free disappeared with the realization that I'd come this far but could still very easily die here. The pounding noise all around me was louder in here, close to deafening.

I spun around and threw my weight as hard as I could against the ventricle, just as it was getting ready to contract. *Wham!* The jolt was agony, and I felt something in my shoulder pop. Pain rippled up through my arm, down my spine.

*Do it again.*

I reared back and hit the wall again. I couldn't tell what was pounding harder, Zooey's heart, or my head. Behind me, her leukocytes were staring at me with a combination of amazement and disbelief.

"What?" I asked. "You've never seen a guy kickstart a girl's heart before?"

The heart muscle contracted again, squeezing like a huge, angry fist, and this time the leukocytes all joined me and we all hit it with everything we had. The impact knocked us back across the ventricle, scattering white blood cells like bowling pins, but I held on.

"Again."

This time nobody argued. They surged around me.

We hit it again.

And again.

And again.

Something was blinking in the corner of my eye,

flashing frantically in an attempt to get my attention, and I realized that it was the digital readout blinking 0:00:00.

I was out of time.

# FORTY-SIX ::: HARLAN

Looking back on it now, I have no idea how I even had the presence of mind to do what I did in those few crucial seconds. All I knew was that at some point, I put my hands together over Zooey's chest, laced my fingers and started pushing on it, counting out loud. Voices were talking behind me, but I didn't hear them. It was like everything else in that dressing room had just disappeared, and I kept doing chest compressions until a hand touched my shoulder. I looked up to see Zooey's dad in front of me.

"I'll take it from here," he said.

I nodded and slumped back while he took over. Zooey's mom was next to him, talking on the phone

while somebody—I realized that it was Shovelhead himself—ran up and gave her something that looked like an
electronic briefcase.

"Here's the AED," he said. "You have to turn it on,
and—"

"I know how it works," Zooey's dad said. He flipped
it open, hitting a red button to activate the defibrillator.
The thing gave a cheerful electronic beep and a digital
voice started talking from somewhere inside the plastic case. It reminded me of the machine that Lenny had

used on himself this morning, which seemed like about a million years ago, and a crazy thought went slingshotting through my head—Zooey's father was going to use Lenny's technology to shrink himself down and go in to save Zooey from the inside.

"It's going to measure her heart rate," Zooey's dad said, unpacking wires and chest-patches from inside the device. "If we can give her an electric shock, we can get her heart rate back to normal sinus rhythm and—"

"Hold on." Zooey's mom felt her pulse again.

"What?"

"She's coming back."

"What? Are you sure?"

"Feel for yourself," she said, and Zooey's dad pressed his fingers against Zooey's throat. For a moment he didn't move, neither of them did . . . and then a wave of relief passed over his face and Zooey's mom's eyes filled with tears.

"Thank God," she said.

Zooey's eyelids twitched and she made a gurgling noise in her chest. She shifted a little and tried to sit up.

"Zooey," her mom said. "Sweetie, it's all right."

Zooey's dad glanced up at me. His face was pale and he didn't look like ex-military anymore. He just looked like somebody's father. "Good job, Harlan," he said.

"Thanks," I nodded back, and flicked my eyes down at Zooey. I knew the truth.

I hadn't done it alone.

# FORTY-SEVEN ::: LENNY

I don't know how I found my way back to the aorta with everything shaking itself to pieces around me, but by the time I got there, I was already aware that it was an extremely tight squeeze. The vessel wall felt like it was closing in, shrinking around me, but I knew that wasn't the case—I was getting bigger. Down in the heart, I had still been the size of a virus, but up here I was already growing larger as the miniaturization process wore off, and within a few seconds I was going to be the biggest problem Zooey Andrews had.

"Dude! You're huge!"

I spun around, caught in the bloodstream, and saw Astro shooting up behind me at top speed. He looked

awestruck and terrified at the same time, as if he thought I might decide to squash him for abandoning me down there.

"I have to get out of here," I said. "Now!"

"Yeah, you think?"

"Exit strategy."

He nodded. "There's an opening somewhere on the face, but you'd better hurry before it clots off."

"Where?"

"Just follow the platelets," he shouted, "but dude, seriously—*go*."

"Astro," I said, hesitating for a moment, just long enough to catch a final glimpse of his face as it melted back into the formless outline of the viral membrane, "thanks."

"Don't mention it, just get moving!"

I jumped into the stream and headed straight up, hurtling through the curves and shooting up the upper vasculature of Zooey's carotid arteries, riding a wave of steadily building pressure that shot me up like a cork from a bottle. With every second I was getting bigger. I knew what would happen if I didn't make it in time—I could end up blocking off the whole artery, cutting off oxygen to the brain. Instead of dying from toxic bacteria, she'd die of an embolic stroke.

I hit the mesh of arterioles in her face, saw the platelets swarming up ahead like a school of jellyfish. When they saw me coming, they burst off in a thousand different directions in sheer terror. I didn't blame them. I went off in their direction as fast as I could, kicking for the surface until I realized that I was looking out at something I hadn't seen in what felt like forever.

Daylight.

## FORTY-EIGHT : : : ZOOEY

The first thing I remember is my dad reaching down to dab the blood from my mouth with his handkerchief. "You split your lip when you fell," he said. "Though right now, that's the least of your worries." He threw the bloody hankie behind the curtain and smiled down at me.

I looked around and saw the EMTs loading up equipment, getting ready to transfer me to the ambulance. Someone had started an IV on my right arm, and there was an oxygen tube in my nose. Monitors were beeping and chirping.

"Hey," I said. "I've got rhythm."

My mom smiled. "You get it from your father."

"What about the play?" I tried to look around. "Is it still happening?"

Nobody said anything. I tried to listen for singing or dialogue from the stage, but that whole part of the world—where I'd dedicated so many weeks and months of my life—seemed to have fallen absolutely silent. As the EMTs lifted the stretcher, I caught a ripple of movement from behind the changing room curtain. I craned my head back, not quite able to believe what I was seeing, sure that it must have been the shock.

Lenny Cyrus was standing there. He was wearing what looked like a tattered scuba diving suit and a cracked face mask, and I thought, *What lake did he crawl out of?*

"Hey, Zooey." He looked as bad as I felt. "Are you all right?"

"I think so." Was I imagining all this? "What are you doing here?"

"I thought of a virus for you."

"Oh yeah? Thanks."

Lenny was saying something else, but I closed my eyes again and let them carry me out.

When I woke up in the hospital that night and saw my mom and dad sitting there by the bed, it all came washing back over me. The fight in the dressing room, the play, the ambulance ride, and the blackness afterward.

"Mom . . ." My voice was a croak. "Dad."

"Hey, look who's awake." She put her iPad aside, and Dad took my hand. "How are you feeling?"

"A little better." I tried to sit up in bed. "Mom, what about the play? Did Aria . . . ?"

She shook her head. "Zooey, after what Aria did to you, you know there was no way anyone was going to let her perform. She's been suspended."

I nodded and tried not to let the disappointment show in my face. "I know, but—"

"Look," she said, "you've got visitors."

I turned and saw Lenny and Harlan standing there on the other side of the room. Harlan had a black eye and was holding a bouquet of flowers, and Lenny had a pink-flowered balloon. I was relieved to see that he wasn't wearing the scuba suit anymore, which maybe meant I'd somehow imagined it all to begin with.

"Sorry." He held out the balloon. "It was all they had in the gift shop."

"Thank you," I said, and looked at Harlan. "Nice shiner, tough guy."

"Thanks," Harlan said. "It's actually gone down a lot in the last hour or so." He took a step closer to my bed. "So the doctor says you're going to be okay."

"That's good."

Lenny came forward. "Prognosis for vibrio vulnificus is really very good. It's actually funny, because estrogen has been shown to have a protective effect against it, and . . ." He caught himself and stopped.

I looked at him. "Why is that funny?"

"It's . . . I mean . . . it's just . . ." He blushed. "You have some pretty rocking estrogen, that's all."

"How would you know?"

Lenny's mouth just tightened as if it had been buttoned up from inside, and he looked at Harlan, who jumped right in to fill the silence. "Mr. Cheney suspended Mick as well as Aria," he said. "I don't think your parents will end up pressing charges, but in my opinion, they totally should. Putting bacteria from that petrie dish into your Diet Coke is attempted murder. I mean, it could've been, if we hadn't gotten to you in time—"

"But you did," I said. "So, thanks. You know, for the whole CPR thing. I think my dad was pretty impressed." I sat back a little. "It's just too bad about the play."

"What about it?" Harlan asked.

"Well, how we had to cancel our first performance."

Harlan and Lenny looked at each other.

"It wasn't canceled," Harlan said.

"I don't understand." My head swiveled back to my mom. "You said we didn't do the play."

"No," Mom said, "I just said that *Aria* wasn't allowed to perform."

"Then, I mean, how did we do it? Who played that role? She was in almost every scene. She had dialogue, songs, choreography to learn . . . Whoever took over would have to have . . ."

"A photographic memory," Lenny said from the foot of the bed. "Yeah. It helps."

I stared at him. "What . . . ?"

"Before we came with you to the hospital," my mom said, "I left my camera with one of the teachers and asked her to take pictures." She handed me her camera. "See for yourself."

I switched it on and stared down at the screen, back up at Lenny, then back down at the screen again. They all gathered around—Harlan, Lenny, and my parents— looking over my shoulder as I started flipping through the pictures. In the first photo, the elves and reindeer were out on stage, performing the opening number. I clicked to the next shot and saw Mrs. Claus coming out into the spotlight in her glittering red gown and boots.

Except this time, the role wasn't played by Aria Keen.

It was Lenny Cyrus, dressed in Aria's costume, with a full face of makeup and a wig.

I stared up at him.

"Lenny?"

He blushed. "Somebody had to do it. I was the only one who could memorize everything on such short notice. So, I stepped in."

"And, actually, he doesn't have a bad voice," Mom said. "Here, keep going."

I clicked through the pictures, through the scenes that I'd written and watched a hundred times in rehearsal. The arrival of the team of scientists and soldiers. The discovery of the elves and reindeer. They all led to the scene that I'd figured out only earlier that day—Harlan's big entrance.

"They got this part on video," Mom said. "Here, press Play."

I stared at the screen, watching as Lenny made his way across the stage in the sequined gown, singing alongside Donnie Delanie as Dr. Henderson and Priscilla Shrewsbury and Tej Singh in their military fatigues, the creepy music swelling, getting more sinister. The canvas set burst open, and Harlan exploded through it into the spotlight in his zombie Santa costume, arms outstretched.

The audience screamed—a huge, loud, totally satisfying scream. Tej and Priscilla swung around and shined their flashlights on Harlan, and the whole scene froze in place.

"Well?" my mom said.

"What can I say?" I reached over and threw my arms around Lenny's neck, giving him a tight squeeze. "You're amazing. You both were."

Lenny blushed again, but he was smiling, and I noticed he still had some eye makeup on that he hadn't been able to scrub off. "It was short notice, but—"

"Lenny, you saved the play."

"I didn't really—"

"Yes, you did. And you . . ."—I turned to Harlan—"saved me." I gave him a hug. "So thank you both."

"No problem." Harlan nodded, but he was staring expectantly at Lenny.

"Zooey, look," Lenny said, with difficulty, "there's something else that we . . ."—he paused—"that I have to tell you." He put on a brave smile. "It's pretty important."

"Okay," I said. "What?"

"What is going on here?" a man said from the doorway. "Leonard?"

Lenny looked over, and when he saw who it was, his smile faded.

"Dad?"

# *FORTY-NINE* : : : *LENNY*

My dad stood in the doorway in his overcoat and boots. He obviously had no intention of coming any further into the room. "Your mother and I would like to talk to you outside."

I didn't move. "You can talk to me right here."

"Excuse me?"

"You heard me." There was a little quaver in my voice, but I got control over it, at least for the moment. "These are my friends. Anything you want to say to me, you can say in front of them."

"Fine," Dad said, straightening up and squaring his shoulders. "We're driving to Aunt Virginia's for the holidays and then taking you straight to Connecticut, to

Brixton Academy. I've already packed your bags. Your mother's waiting in the car."

I glanced back at Harlan, then Zooey and her parents as my dad, the world-renowned Nobel Prize–winning scientist Donald Cyrus, stood waiting for his son to obey orders.

"Wait," I said.

"What?"

"Dad, I did something today, and I need to tell you about it." I glanced back at Zooey. "All of you."

"Leonard, this is no time for—"

"Everything I told you this morning was true," I said. "I really did shrink myself down to the molecular level. Harlan dropped me in Zooey's Diet Coke, and she swallowed me, and I spent the day traveling around inside her body, trying to get to her brain. At one point I made her say she had chromoblastomycosis." I looked at Zooey again. "Sorry about that."

Zooey and her parents were staring at me blankly with something that wasn't even shock. It was more like total incomprehension. I turned back to my dad, took in another breath, and continued.

"Anyway, I didn't have any idea that Mick and Aria had already slipped that bacteria in her soda when I went inside . . . but it was probably a good thing that I was there, because I helped save her life. Have you ever seen *vibrio vulnificus* up close?" I shook my head.

"It's pretty hideous."

My dad scowled. "Harlan said—"

"Harlan was just trying to protect me," I said. "That's why he told you that it was all a joke. I was mad at him at the time, but now I realize that he was only trying to help."

"But he came back to the house later," Dad said, "and told us it was all true."

"You did?" I glanced at Harlan. "Why?"

"I thought they'd listen," Harlan said. "I wanted them to know the truth."

"Yeah," I said. "That was . . . probably a good idea." I turned back to look at Zooey again, and this time I made myself stare straight into her eyes. "The point is, I was wrong about everything, and Harlan was right. Zooey's a person, not a science experiment. I might have been inside her heart, but I don't really know her at all—and I don't deserve to. Zooey, I'm sorry."

"Wait a second," Mr. Andrews said. "I'm a little confused here. When you say you were inside my daughter's heart, you're speaking metaphorically, right?"

"No, sir," I said. "I mean that I was actually inside the left ventricle."

"The left . . ." Mr. Andrews looked at his wife, then back at me. "I don't understand. Was this part of the play?"

"I'm not sure." Zooey's mom glanced at the camera. "She didn't tape that part."

"Well, it's not important," Mr. Andrews said. "What matters is that Zooey's going to be fine." He stood up and walked over to my father, holding out his hand. "I'm Robert Andrews, by the way, Zooey's father. This is my wife, Laura." He beamed at me. "Quite a boy you've got there."

"Thank you." My dad allowed his hand to be pumped twice up and down, but his eyes never left mine. Behind the lenses of his glasses, he seemed incapable of so much as a blink.

"We're going down to the cafeteria to get a cup of coffee if you and your wife want to join us," Zooey's dad said. "Give the kids a little privacy before visiting hours are over. It's been quite a day."

"I-I'll . . . just . . ." My dad just looked at me. "My wife and I . . ."

"Great," Mr. Andrews said. "See you shortly."

When he and Zooey's mom left, my dad turned back to me. He was quiet for what felt like a very long time, and the only noise was the steady beep of Zooey's heart monitor from the corner of the room.

"Look, Dad," I said. "You don't have to say anything. I get it. I messed up today, bigtime. And if you and Mom still want to send me to Brixton—"

"Lenny, come here." He leaned forward and gave me a hug, squeezing me tightly. "Son, I'm so proud of you."

"What?" I drew back, so stunned that I was sure I'd misheard what he'd said. "You're not mad?"

"When you first told me this morning," he said, "I was in shock. I simply couldn't believe it. And then when I thought you'd made the whole thing up, I was angry . . . but I suppose some part of me was also relieved. The idea of my own son succeeding where I had failed . . ." He shook his head. "Lenny, what you did today will change the annals of scientific history forever. If your mother and I send you off to Brixton, how would we ever help you develop this technology's true potential?"

"You . . . want to help me?"

"Of course," he said. "If it's all right with you."

I looked at him and smiled. "Yeah," I said. "I'd like that."

"Good. When you get home tonight, we'll sit down and go over all of it, step by step. I want to hear everything you did from the very beginning. Your mother will want to hear it too."

"Okay."

"Excellent." He clapped me on the back, and turned to Harlan and Zooey. "Good to see you both again. You should come by the house sometime, Zooey."

When he left, Harlan frowned at me. "Did he just say *annals?*"

"Hey." I sat down in front of Zooey, whose expression hadn't changed since I'd told her about what really happened today. "You're . . . probably pretty angry right now, huh?"

She glared at me. "*Yes.* I mean . . ." She paused. "No. I don't know." She reached back and tucked a strand of hair back behind her eyes. "Is that all true, Lenny? What you did?"

"Yeah."

"You actually dropped down into my stomach and traveled through my whole body to my brain, all so you could get to know me better?"

"Uh-huh."

"Wow." She just stared at me for a long moment. "All this time, I thought you were supposed to be *smart*."

"Yeah, well," I said, "I guess you didn't really know me any better than I knew you."

She reached over and squeezed my hand. "You are aware that there are other ways of becoming some-body's friend, right?"

"I get it," I said. "Harlan deserves you more than I do."

"What?" Harlan sat up, blushing. "Nobody said—"

"*Deserves* me?" Zooey cut in, taking her hand back.

"When I was in your brain," I said, "I saw how much you think about him. It's pretty obvious you like him."

"Lenny . . ." She smiled. "Harlan's my friend. Friends think about each other."

"So that's all he is, a friend?"

"That's *what* he is," Zooey said. "You, too. And I don't have to choose between either you because I've already chosen both of you—as friends. Got it?"

"Okay," I said. "I guess I can live with that."

"Good, because you're going to have to. I'm not even allowed to date until high school anyway."

We all sat there without talking for a second, and then she said, "I do have one question . . . When you were floating around inside of me—I mean, what did I look like?"

"What did you *look* like?"

"You know, from the inside," she said. "I mean, all those veins and glands and everything. Was it gross?"

"Zooey," I said, "please. We're talking about the opportunity to witness the miracle of human physiological interaction on the molecular level. It was . . ." I glanced up at her. "It was pretty gross."

She smiled. "I'd hate to see what *you* look like inside."

"Maybe you'll get a chance," I said. "Maybe next time—"

"Oh, no," Harlan said. "Never again, Lenny, seriously."

"No, I was thinking, what if we reversed the process?"

"Reversed?" Zooey asked.

"Sure. You know—*increased* Planck's Constant. Increased everything on the molecular level. I mean, it stands to reason . . ." I looked up. "What, too soon?"

Harlan and Zooey were both staring at me, but the idea was already taking shape in my head, and I could tell right away that it wasn't just going to be big.

It was going to be *huge*.